CHRISTMAS LANE

Sweet Christmas Series Volume 6

SAMANTHA JACOBEY

Lavish Publishing LLC

First Edition

Sweet Christmas Series book 6

2020 Lavish Publishing, LLC

All Rights Reserved

Published in the United States by Lavish Publishing, LLC, Midland, TX

Cover Design by: Victor R. Sosa

Cover Images: CanStock Photo

Paperback Edition

ISBN: 978-1-64900-007-1

Contents

Prologue   1
1. Uncertain Times   7
2. Birthday Girl   13
3. Untraditional   21
4. A Happy Tune   29
5. Let It Snow   39
6. Darkness Falls   47
7. In the Shadow   53
8. Secrets and Surprises   63
9. Confront and Confess   71
10. House of Plenty   77
11. Ring the Bells   83
12. New Arrival   93
13. What Friends Are For   99
14. What's in a Name   105
15. A Toast to 2020   111
Epilogue   123

Thank You   127
About the Author   129
Also by SAMANTHA JACOBEY   131
Also from the Lavish Family   133

Prologue

"CAROL!" Holly called loudly. Standing in their kitchen, she rolled her eyes to glare at the ceiling above her. "No answer," she muttered. Wiping her hands on a towel, she left the remaining dishes to soak.

The stairs creaking beneath her steps, her finger-tips trailed along the smooth wood of the banister, its fine craftsmanship soothing her ruffled disposition. The girls loved their house, after all, and for a moment her mind flitted back to the day Gerald Ford had taken them on a tour of the enormous dwelling. A smile teasing her lips as she reached the second-floor landing, she steeled her nerves to face her partner.

"Caroline?" Her voice calmer, Holly inched forward, her feet sliding slightly across the glossy hard wood of the hallway. Reaching the far end, she hesitated, the shape of a woman darkened by the bright light of the window before her. "Baby, are you ok?" she rasped as she eased into the room.

"It should have rained," Carol huffed, her breathing ragged. Her fingertips swiped at her cheeks, removing drops of sadness while her eyes remained fixed on the scene below.

Outside, warm sunshine illuminated the freshly trimmed grass of their sizable yard. On the far side, a gentle breeze disturbed the roses, causing them to dance. "It's too beautiful," she sighed, imagining the rows of chairs and the arch she longed to stand beneath.

Reaching her, Holly's hand started at the small of her lover's back, her fingers kneading firmly as they worked their way up. At least two inches shorter, she gave a firm squeeze at the top, then rested her cheek against a warm shoulder blade. "Our day will come, Love."

Carol sputtered a muted reply, then twisted to slide an arm around the other girl's waist. Drawing her forward to stand beside her, she pointed. "I think the placement will be perfect, but we will definitely want an awning for the dancefloor."

Holly winced, her mood sinking. "You're holding out for a summer wedding, then?" Her heart heavy, she felt the strain of losing an entire year…another year.

"Of course," Caroline coughed, squeezing as she elaborated. "I'm going to marry you beneath a bright, warm sun. Out in the open for all the world to see. If I have to wait a full year to see our matching gowns, well…" Her voice trailed away as she bent slightly, her lips grazing the warmth of Holly's,

"We'll just have to watch our figures so they still fit," she teased.

The flutter within her chest giving her courage, Holly blurted, "I've done something." Her eyes flicking between Carol's stern gaze and the lush lips she had just tasted, she added, "Please, don't be mad."

Her hands dropping, Carol stepped back. When an explanation did not come, she folded her arms across her chest.

"I just got off the phone, actually," Holly gushed, her anxiety uncharacteristic of her. As the sturdy and level-headed member of their relationship, she tightened her jaw. "I was talking to Ben."

"Ben." Carol's brow knitted in confusion, expecting some connection to their postponed nuptials. "That's a bit random. What did he want?"

"He's lonely, I think," Holly blurted. "You know he lives alone. No family close by, no friends to hang out with due to current circumstances."

"Uh-huh."

"I offered him a room." Her words tumbled out, a thick silence hanging in the air when her lips pressed shut.

"A room!" Carol shrieked. Taking a step back, she glanced out the window, the bright sun below suddenly too much. "Why would you do such a thing?"

"I thought the two of you were friends," Holly defended, squaring her small frame. "Ben needs us. And we have plenty of rooms!"

She glanced around the room's bare walls, the one

they occupied held a chair, a table and a lamp, then muttered with a sigh, "I told Gary it was too much house for us."

"Oh, baby." Holly laughed, closing the distance between them and wrapping her arms around her best friend. "I love you so much."

"I love you, too," Carol spat, "but you could have at least asked me before you invited someone to come live with us." Her mind jerking to the obvious, she demanded, "And why is he coming anyways? It's not like he can't afford his place."

"I told you, he's lonely. They've had courts suspended for months. He has nothing to do and no one to talk to."

"So, you thought it would be any different over here? We still have jobs, Holly."

"He can manage the roses," the other woman teased, snuggling against Carol's chest. "Please say yes."

"Do I have a choice?" Caroline demanded, her voice still gruff.

Grinning, Holly sighed. "Thank you. I'll let you pick which room he gets."

"Well, obviously it won't be this one," Carol sniffed.

"What's wrong with this one?" Holly gasped, stepping back to turn and inspect the room for herself.

"It doesn't have a bathroom, silly. We can't have him wandering around with his man-parts hanging out, now can we?"

Holly laughed aloud at the thought of it. "We can

give him the one on the front of the house, with a full bath."

"Exactly," Carol agreed with a firm nod. Her eyes drawn to the window, her lips curled into a lopsided grin. "You aren't charging him rent, are you?"

"I told him he could chip in. I didn't specify how much."

"Good." Carol's lips curled deviously. "It might be kind of fun to boss him around for a change."

Rolling her tongue as she picked up on her lover's dark humor, Holly agreed, "We'll have plenty for him to do around here, I'm sure."

ONE

Uncertain Times

GLANCING down at the phone resting on her knee, Candy smiled and accepted the call. "Hello?"

"Hey, Sunshine!"

"Hi, Cat."

"How are things going with the little momma?" Catherine Douglas had a musical quality to her voice, its warm tones drifted out of the device. "Am I on speaker?"

"Yes, you are," Candy replied with a giggle.

"Oh, are you busy?" Cathy paused. "Hello?"

"I'm just tired," Candy confessed, resting her chin on the back of the couch, her eyes still fixed on the man across the street. "I'm sitting here watching Benjamin Monroe trim the girls' shrubs."

"And you don't have the strength to hold your phone to your ear," Cathy mocked.

"Something like that."

"So, how is Ben doing? He's been there a couple of months, hasn't he?"

"About a month, I guess," Candy replied. "He was a little depressed when he moved in. Everything from his law firm went into storage. He's doing ok now, I think. We all are, I guess." The sadness creeping into her voice, she made no attempt to hide it.

"Hey, don't go there!" Cathy challenged. "How are things with Daks? Are you going to let him go live or is he doing the distance learning?"

"The school is offering distance, so we are taking them up on that. We have too many weakened bodies around here to risk the exposure." Her fingertips traced the line of her belly. She wasn't big yet, but the bulge was more pronounced than she could recall ever being with her eldest son. "Did I tell you it's a boy?"

"No, you didn't! How wonderful! Is he going to be Gerald Junior?"

Candy cringed. "Not if I can help it. I still can't believe I'm due on Christmas Day." Her voice quavered, exposing her apprehension.

"Oh, come on, girlfriend. Don't be like that. Christmas has been really good to you these last few years."

"I know. That's why I'm waiting for the one that will get me." Candy laughed loudly, hearing the words that sounded so absurd, even to her own ears. Inhaling deeply, she continued to rub as if caressing the tiny body inside her. Exhaling her breath through puckered lips, she tried again. "I'm in a good place. Our family is well, and we can do this."

"That's my girl," Cathy rallied. "How was registration? I'll be so glad when we both finally finish."

"All online. They offered an in-person lab, but I changed to another course to avoid it. Maybe I'll take it in the spring, or even next fall if we have to wait that long for the pandemic to end."

"It will end," her friend assured. "We just have to be strong and do what we should until the vaccine is here and ready."

Candy rolled her eyes. "This is all we ever talk about these days." *All anyone talks about.*

"Well, I'm *trying* to talk about something else. Are you guys making plans for Joy's birthday yet? I know it's still six weeks out, but it can't hurt to have a plan."

Candy sighed loudly. "Yes, we are going to have a small gathering of the bubble, and send a Zoom link to those who want to join us." *Everything leads back to the quarantine.*

"Oh, Candy," Cathy lamented. "I know this is hard. We really are going to get through these uncertain times. I promise."

"I know. Hey!" Candy sat straight up, remembering more news to share. "Carol said it would be ok if you wanted to come and join the bubble for the big event. They are only letting one person in the hospital, though, so you'll have to fight Gary for the role of support person."

Giggling filled the air of the living room, and for a moment both girls forgot about the months of stress. Catching her breath, Candy's best friend soothed, "I'll think about it," knowing full well she would never even attempt to depose Gary from his rightful position. "Right now, I have to worry about this semester. You would think learning online should somehow be easier, but I swear it was twice as hard. I need to get things in order if I'm going to have a successful semester."

"Me too," Candy sighed, returning to the moment. "Thanks, Cathy."

"For what, babe?"

"For being my friend, even with all my little issues." Candice Ford made light of her mental state, fully aware of the burden it sometimes placed on others. "It means a lot that you're here for me."

"It means a lot to me, too," Cathy stated firmly. "You have my number, so make sure you call me with any and all news —good and bad."

"I will. Bye," Candy sniffed, quickly cutting off the device before the sound of her tears reached the other side.

"Are you ok?" Carol asked.

Candy jumped at the voice, her phone sliding off her lap and becoming wedged between the cushions. "I thought you were shopping," she snapped as she rummaged around to retrieve it.

"I just got home," Caroline explained as she set down a large bag. "I guess you didn't hear me come in or see me in the driveway." She dropped it there, aware Candy was still her boss and under no obligation to help carry the groceries.

"I must have blanked it out." Pulling out the

Android, she made sure the call had properly ended. "I was talking to Cathy."

"I heard," Carol snipped. "Is she going to come and join our bubble?"

"She doesn't know yet. She's got a class that meets in person, I think." Getting to her feet, Candy joined the taller woman in the kitchen and began to help unpack the groceries. Above them, the ceiling creaked, followed by the sound of tiny feet pattering across the floor of her room.

A smile spreading across her face, Candy called over her shoulder as she started up the stairs, "I got it."

Watching her disappear, Caroline chuckled to herself. She had overheard the tail end of the phone call and had to agree, Candy had her issues and being pregnant didn't help them, but Joylana could always put her employer in a better mood.

Picking up one of the sacks, Caroline flicked on the light and opened the door to the basement to head below.

TWO

Birthday Girl

"WHOA-HO-HO," Gerald Ford sang out as he entered the kitchen. On his shoulders sat his princess, her ebony hands pressed against his head as she held on, the air filled with peals of laughter.

Sitting at the table, a fat crayon in his hand, Dakota cackled, "Joy'ana ridin'."

"She sure is," Candy agreed. "Wanna help momma clear off the table for the cake?"

Slapping the book closed, color still inside, Daks leapt to his feet without a reply. Instead, he scooped up everything he could carry and darted into Lanelle's room. "Wake up, Mimi! It's cake!" he announced to the prone figure beneath her blankets.

"I'm awake," Candy's mother slurred.

Entering from the adjoining bath, Holly advised, "Daks, put your things on the round table, please. Lanelle, let me help you into your bath before we do the cake." Providing leverage, they got her up into a sitting position and she added, "There we go."

From the doorway, Candy watched the process. Her hand resting on her belly, she fought to stifle her fears, choosing to focus on the happy occasion. Her mother's health loomed like a dark cloud that constantly hovered in the back of her mind, but today it would not get the better of her if she could help it.

"I've got the cake," Carol offered as she applied a damp rag to the tabletop. "Who wants to set up the Zoom?"

For a moment, everyone paused, their eyes darting around at one another.

"Not me." Ben laughed. "I'm holding down this chair." He folded his hands on the flat surface, ready to face them down.

Finally, Candy rolled her eyes and sighed in an exaggerated fashion, "Fine. I'll get the laptop." For the most part, it was Gary's family who would be joining them via the connection, but she knew he deserved time with Joy. Not really a chore, he reveled in tending to her, especially on her second birthday.

Placing the squirming toddler in her highchair, Gary beamed. He had been at the station the day her birth mother had left her in their secured box. He had been the one to unwrap her frail body and discovered the handwritten note penned by the woman who knew letting Joy go gave her a better chance at life. A better life he would do everything in his power to fulfill. "Thanks, Kitten," he murmured to Candy as she moved past them. His wife had been less gracious about his wanting to adopt than he could have hoped but, knowing her emotional challenges, he felt grateful she had made the choice, even if she didn't enjoy it.

Stomping down to the office, Candy gathered the computer and returned to the kitchen, where everyone else busily prepared the scene. Once she established the connection, she used her phone to text the code to the list of guests they had chosen to invite. Watching as the screen populated with friendly faces, she grimaced, then forced a smile as she moved into the range of the camera. "Hi guys!" she called cheerfully, adding a wave for effect. She had gotten better at pretending, or at least she hoped she had.

"Where's the birthday girl?" Eve snorted, obviously miffed about something.

"We're almost ready," Candy replied soothingly. Glancing around, she adjusted the position of the laptop to improve their view. "Can you see now?"

"That's much better," Roger announced, wiggling in his seat.

"Be still," Eve commanded as he squirmed in the chair beside her.

"Shh," he hushed back.

Candy resisted the urge to mute them.

"I think we're all set," Gary announced. Using a long arm to slide the cake closer, he fumbled in his pocket for a lighter. Once the dancing flames glowed before them, he pulled away as singing filled the air. When the song ended, he instructed, "Blow it hard, Joy!"

They had been practicing all week, preparing her for the big moment. Her cheeks puffed out, air hissed between her tiny, puckered lips, and the flames fluttered to the side. Not satisfied with the result, she inhaled deeply and tried again, this time succeeding in extinguishing the pair of candles and sending a thin line of smoke curling above them. "Yay!" she cheered, clapping her hands as the others joined in the celebration.

Glancing at the screen, Gary could see his father genuinely enjoying the moment. His mother on the other hand appeared to be chewing sour grapes. Sighing deeply, he did his best to appease her. "Can you see all right, Mother?"

"I see fine," she quibbled, dabbing the corner of her eye. "From here."

A joyous crescendo of laughter filled the air and Gary nodded knowingly. "I know, Mother," he stated flatly. Dropping the conversation there, he turned to the cake and began cutting small squares. "Do we have ice cream?"

"Yes," Carol replied, opening the freezer and pulling out a large container. "I remembered."

Holding out a bowl, Ben offered, "I guess I'll help with the serving. Might as well make myself useful." He winked at Candy, knowing she probably needed a break after the computer.

"Thanks, Ben." Gary placed a square of cake into the dish, then returned to snag another cube of decadence. "This cake looks delicious, Kitten."

Her face flushed and Candy beamed. She had been taking an online decorating class during the quarantine and creating the special desert had certainly raised her spirits. "Thank you, Babe," she replied meekly.

After a few minutes, the noise level dropped as everyone enjoyed their slices and scoops. Glancing at the Zoom, Gary could see that the Doubletrees and other cousins had provided a cake for themselves, as had Cathy, but his parents simply sat in their chairs… glaring at them. "Where's your cake, Dad?"

"We don't need cake," Eveline tartly replied.

Licking at the icing coating the roof of his mouth, Gary considered his reply. Nothing he could say would appease her. "This really isn't the time," he said instead. "You know we are going to arrange things for Halloween. You'll get to see everyone then."

"Hmph," Eve grunted, crossing her arms over her chest.

"Please don't," Candy begged through gritted teeth.

"Exactly," Gary inserted, aware that everyone had been drawn into the turmoil that zoomed across the airwaves for the whole family to see. "I promise, Mother. We will see you in person in a few days." Without hesitating, he reached over and removed them from the connection.

"What did you do that for?" Candy squealed, terrified at what Eveline Ford would say or do next.

"Shh," Gary shushed her. "Enjoy your daughter's birthday and let me handle my mother." Placing his bowl on the table, he stood and marched out of the room, turning left towards the office.

Around her, spoons clanging against dishes filled the small space. Standing frozen in place, she waited, not entirely sure what to do, but the others dropped the confrontation and focused on the celebration.

"I have to hand it to you, Candy, this cake is delicious," Cathy piped up, holding up her plate as she took an exaggerated forkful. She had baked a double chocolate cake for herself that very morning.

"Oh, isn't it heavenly?!" Anette agreed, offering her bite to the camera for the others to see. "Isn't it lovely how we all get to have our favorite this way?"

For a moment, Candy thought she might cry, but Joy's dimples creased her tiny face as she sat beaming at her and her heart melted. "Oh, guys. I so wish you could be here."

"We are here," Paula clipped, "as much as we can be. You and Gary have genuine concerns for the well-being of your family. Don't apologize for that. Eve will simply have to respect it."

"Well said," Robert agreed next to her. "This is Joylana's day. Don't let anyone spoil it."

Nodding, Candy placed her bowl on the table beside her husband's and followed him down the hall. Pausing at the door, she could hear his stern voice on the other side.

"I understand, Mother, but you have to also understand. Just because you don't think there is any danger in a visit doesn't negate how we feel about it."

Candy couldn't hear her response.

"Yes, I know that I'm still working and that does raise some risk of exposure," he continued, catching a shadow in the hallway. "We are taking precautions for that."

Realizing she'd been noticed, Candy stepped through the portal. "We can talk about this later," she announced loudly. "Come and join us."

Her simple request spoke volumes. "I have to go, Mother," Gary cut off Eve's rant. "I'll call you tomorrow and give you the details for Halloween." Removing the phone from his ear and ending the call, he placed the phone on his desk. Following Candy back to the kitchen, they both wore smiles as they rejoined the group of happy guests, both live and virtual, all of them ignoring the problems of the world as best they could.

"That's it," Roger announced firmly. "Party's over."

"That is not it," Eve countered, pressing her phone firmly against her ear. Across town, Gary's device sat on his desk, flashing brightly in the darkened room. "Damn it," she cursed as his voicemail cut in for the umpteenth time.

His hand shaking slightly, Roger gently removed her fingers to take possession of her iPhone. "Eve, listen to me. I know how stubborn you can be, but our son can be just as hardheaded as you. Look how long it took him to settle down and give us those grandchildren you were always harping about. And now he's got a beautiful family, and there's even a new baby on the way."

"For all the good it does me," Eve retorted. "I haven't seen or touched them in months." She wafted her hands around her. "Not since this virus thing started."

"Exactly," Roger agreed. "And it's our son's job to keep that family of his safe. He thinks this bubble of theirs is the way to do that."

"Such nonsense," she spat, pursing her lips.

"Hey, I watch the news," her husband pointed out. "The cases here are rising. Cases pretty much everywhere, for that matter. I don't know how much nonsense that it is, and I don't really care. What I do know is that you aren't getting anywhere until you agree to Gary's terms. And quite frankly, I'm tired of you antagonizing him over it." He lifted his chin as he spoke, as if preparing for a punch.

"I do not antagonize," Eveline snapped, her deep brown eyes sharp as daggers.

"I'm not going to argue with you on that either," Roger replied with a chuckle. "I'm going up those stairs and I'm packing a bag. I'm not leaving this house again until Halloween. I'm going to wear my mask, I'm going to behave myself, and if I'm lucky, I'll be able to hug my grandchildren again a few days after that."

"You wouldn't," Eve fumed. "You wouldn't dare take his side!"

"You can't win this, Eve," he called over his shoulder as he reached the first step. "There are no winners here, really. We're either all on the same team or we don't get to play."

THREE

Untraditional

SITTING beside her husband in his sedan, Eve held a napkin in her left hand. As her thoughts turned, she twisted it, squeezing to compress it as much as she could, then releasing it to watch its slow expanse. "You know everything we are going to miss," she sniveled.

"I know," Roger replied.

"Um-hmph," she grunted.

Turning the car into the narrow drive, Roger slowed the vehicle to a crawl as he examined the hefty structure. The house had been in their family for a century but it had not been altered in decades, at least until now. Easing off the brake, he edged around to the back of the house, taking an empty spot furthest from the commotion in the back yard. "Put your mask on," he instructed.

A white cloth version, Eve placed the strap over her left ear, then the right. Adjusting it, she muttered, "I hate this."

"Think of your granddaughter. You won't hate it so much." Opening the door, he left her to her fuming. A cold blast of air rustled his hair and he grinned behind his dark square of cloth. Reaching the porch and walking up the new ramp, he pointed at it. "At least it keeps your face warm."

"That it does," Gary affirmed cheerily. He wore a bright orange cover with a jack-o-lantern face. "It's good to see you, Dad."

"Yeah." Roger shoved his hands in his pockets. "I guess we are confined to the porch?"

"Please." Looking past his father, Gary could see Eve still seated inside the car. "Damn, that woman is stubborn." He stopped there, knowing any more would be futile.

The back door swung open and Daks bolted outside. "Hey, Grampa," he called as he dashed for the swings.

"We set this up for you," Gary instructed, indicating a square folding table on the end of the row. "You can have a seat and one of the girls will serve you."

Taking the chair next to the railing, Roger reserved the one next to the house for his wife, should she decide to join him. "This is hard for her, son."

Blinking a few times, Gary nodded. He'd been married to Candy for four years. It surprised him how much that relationship had taught him about his mother. "She'll come around." Candy and Eve were more alike than either one of them would ever admit.

Behind him, the door swung open again as Candy

and Carol began to bring out food. Ben followed behind, ready to help with the Zoom.

"Benjamin, how long have you been living here now?" Roger called loudly to overpower his mask.

"I live in the house across the street, actually. With the girls. They let me have a nice room all to myself back in July." He played up the experience, well aware the girls had a room for Eve and Roger as well, should they ever decide to accept it. He had helped with the furnishing and had taken on several new hobbies and interests since moving in. "It's nice to have a place away from everything and still have friends around."

"You like being isolated like that?" Eve interrupted, having joined them.

"That's a nice mask you have there, Mrs. Ford," Ben offered rather than argue, swallowing as he recalled the few times he had worked for her. Tough as nails would be the phrase he thought best described her.

"I'm sure it is," she grumbled, taking the seat Roger held out for her.

"Yes, well…" Ben stammered. Rubbing his hands together, he turned back to his task and soon had the cousins populating the screen.

Calling Daks over to their long picnic style table, Candy helped Joylana into her booster seat. Her laughter and playfulness took Eve's breath away and she felt foolish at the way she had behaved by the end of the meal.

"I didn't bring a suitcase," she grumbled from behind her glass of wine.

"Sure you did," Roger informed her with a sly grin.

"What's in it?"

"Socks. Underwear. A few changes of clothes. I figure we'll order anything we need and have it delivered." He grinned at his bride, thankful she had started to make sense of their situation. "We'll be safe here, too, Eve."

"We were safe at home."

"Ok, we'll be just as safe here, but with benefits." He could imagine the afternoons of play already.

"Are you two ready for dessert?" Carol asked as she approached their space, taking care to maintain her distance.

"Sure," Roger called with a nod, then added, "I hear that house of yours is filled with bedrooms."

"Yes, sir." She smiled. "One of them if made up for you, if you are ready to have it."

Eve's jaw dropped, and she quickly clamped it shut. Did none of them believe she would get her way?

"That'll be fine," Roger observed, a low gravelly laugh escaping him at his wife's expression. "And we'll take the room."

"That's good news," Gary called from across the wooden slats holding his plate. "You'll have to quarantine, though. Fourteen days."

"We started on Joy's birthday," Eveline sniffed, clearly defeated.

"Oh. Then it will be less," Gary observed with a boisterous laugh. Turning to his daughter, who currently snuggled on Lanelle's lap, he raised his glass in a toast. "You hear that princess? Grandmother and Grampa are finally coming to stay."

Joy only giggled, curling into the warm blanket that kept out the cool evening air.

A few hours later, Gary donned his mask as he and Roger carried the suitcases Roger had packed for their exile. "I'm really glad you decide to join us, Dad. I really am."

"I'm glad, too, son. It was your mother who needed convincing."

"Yeah, I know that's right," Gary muttered.

"The house looks good, by the way." Roger indicated over his shoulder, pointing out the ramp that had been added to the front. "I guess having one on both sides must have cost you a pretty penny."

"It wasn't cheap," Gary agreed, reaching the back door of Carol and Holly's home and sliding it open for them. "We are having one built over here next week, if we can beat the snow."

"Do you think you'll need one here? Surely Lanelle doesn't spend time over here when everything is suited for her at home."

"We want her to have the option. It's better for her to maintain her mobility."

"I guess that makes sense." Roger contemplated the notion. Climbing the stairs, he observed, "Seems like the girls are starting a retirement community over here."

"Only until the pandemic is over," Gary countered. "After that, we all go back to our lives, same as they were."

"Our lives will never be the same as they were," Roger warned. "You may not see it now, but our world has changed. The way we talk to people. The way we spend time with people. Hell, the way we shop and eat. Pretty much everything will be different in one way or another."

Gary nodded thoughtfully. "Perhaps, but I'd like to think we can hold onto who we are at least."

"That'll change, too," Roger wheezed, winded from the climb. Placing his suitcase on the bed, he looked around the room. Across the covers, he could see a cozy sitting area arranged in front of the small window, complete with two chairs and a coffee table. To the left of it, a narrow door presumably led to their private bath. "The closet is small," he observed.

"Well, we can't really help that," Gary chided. "I'm sure you and Mother will be comfortable at any rate."

"Indeed." Roger paused, sizing his son up. "You've become quite a man, Gerald. I'm proud of you. Thank you for inviting us here and making us part of your bubble."

His lips twisting in an odd pucker, Gary considered his reply. "I'm not sure how to take that, Dad."

"Genuinely, I assure you," Roger supplied, grinning behind the mask he had almost forgotten that he wore. "When we finish our quarantine, I'll give you a hug."

Gary chuckled at the thought of it. "We've never really been huggers, Dad."

"Well, it's never too late to start," the older man assured.

FOUR

A Happy Tune
———————————————

"I'M SORRY, Kitten. I have to go when I can get in," Gary offered. Taking a sip from his steaming cup, he anxiously awaited her reply.

"I know," his wife mumbled, stirring her bowl of cereal listlessly. "Maybe I can take the bus."

Carol gasped, reminding them they were not alone.

Candy cut her eyes over at their housekeeper and near live-in nanny. "I don't want to drive," she defended.

"Maybe Dad could drive you," her mate offered with a hopeful tone. "I'm sure he wouldn't mind."

"Ben might be willing," Carol dared to add, aware they weren't really speaking to her.

"There's an idea," Gary agreed, lifting his mug in a mock toast. "He's a good driver, and I'm sure his car would be nice and cozy. Far better than the bus."

"I suppose," Candy agreed dejectedly.

"I'll give him a call before I head out," Gary

stated firmly. Rising from his chair, he sauntered down the hall to his office.

"What's up?" Ben cut to the chase when answering the ring.

"Good morning!" Gary replied with a hearty laugh. In the last few months, their family dynamic had changed drastically. Benjamin Monroe had been little more than a family acquaintance before the pandemic, but now he mowed the grass and ran errands for the growing group they affectionately referred to as "The Bubble".

Ben echoed the warm greeting. "Well, you're in cheery mood."

"Yes and no. Candy's appointment is this morning and I have to go downtown to see about taking that leave of absence."

"Oh, they're both today?" Ben mused, seeing the conflict.

"Yes. Could you take Candy to Dr. Castleberry's office? She doesn't want to drive, and I don't think the bus is a good option."

"Certainly not," Ben echoed the sentiment. "I'm here for you, buddy. Tell Candy I'll be ready. What time?"

"She's supposed to be there at ten-thirty, so I would plan to get there right on time. Otherwise, they'll make you wait in the car," Gerald advised. "And thanks."

Ending the call, Gary pursed his lips at the device, considering canceling his appointment with his boss. However, he knew if he were able to take the time off, this would be his best opportunity to make a little lemonade out of the huge pile of lemons the quarantine had been serving up.

Returning to the kitchen, he called cheerfully, "You're in luck, Kitten. Ben is all set to have you there at ten-thirty on the button."

Candy cut her eyes up at him, catching the strain on his rugged features he worked so hard to hide. Taking pity on him, she lifted her chin and smiled. "Thank you. We'll be fine." Resting her hand on her belly, she indicated the "we" she spoke of and her grin grew wide. "Have you talked to your mother about the name?"

"No," Gary moaned in an exaggerated fashion as he reclaimed his seat. "You know she has her heart set on Gerald Ford Junior."

"I know, but it sounds so…stuffy."

"I think it sounds rather redneck, if you ask me," Gary countered. "Junior," he drawled.

Carol's laugher tinkled from the sink. Unable to resist, she selected a towel to dry her hands and turned to face them. Leaning back against the cabinets, she mused, "What if you used another term instead of junior, like maybe the second? That would be almost the same thing."

Candice cut her eyes over at her. "I doubt Eve would let us get away with that. You know how she is when she gets an idea in her head."

"Yes, we know exactly how she is," Gary clarified without adding the obvious conclusion. "We still have a few weeks, Kitten. It will work out." Rising, he went to gather his coat. "I have no idea how long I'll be, so don't wait lunch on me, but I will definitely be home for dinner."

Carol nodded. "I'll be making steaks tonight."

"Sounds good," Gary called over his shoulder as he made his way out the door.

"I should get dressed," Candy admitted with a sigh. On her feet, she used the table to steady herself, Carol observed the sway in her small frame.

"Are you ok?" Caroline asked. "Should I call Holly?"

"No, I'm fine." Candy released the table and took a step back to demonstrate her composure. "I just stood up too fast." Making a break for it, she hurriedly took to the stairs. Glancing at the clock, she had over an hour and decided a nice soak before their departure would be in order.

"Turn left here," Candy advised. Next to her, Ben guided his black BMW along the sparsely populated streets. With the new stay-at-home orders, few people ventured out in the uncertain times.

Benjamin grinned back at her. "Right on time, my lady." He glanced around the deserted parking lot. "Are you sure they are seeing patients today?"

"Yes," Candy snapped, instantly regretting it. "Everything is pandemic driven. Only those who have to be here come in, and since I'm high risk, it's even more changed." She used her mask to cover her concern. These days, she worried constantly about developing eclampsia with her second child, just as she had the first. Every little symptom ate at her, and this morning the burden of it was almost more than she could bear.

"I see," he observed, not sure that he really did. Candy had been behaving strangely as of late, and he wished like hell one of them could help her out of her funk. Climbing out, he walked around and opened the door for her.

"I can walk by myself." She held her tone in check this time, still put out at the whole situation.

"Not on this blacktop parking lot. You fall on a patch of ice, I would never forgive myself." His words sending gentle puffs of steam around his mask, his tenderness swayed her.

"I'm sorry, Ben. You're a good friend to bring me here. And to see me to the door." Taking his arm, she felt the slick spots as they made their way to the door, gripping him a little tighter at the thought of taking that tumble he has spoken of. "Too bad we don't get handicapped parking," she observed with a loud laugh. Large patches of snow dotted the ground. "Looks like the weather is going to turn before we get out of here."

"Yes, that would be nice on a day like today," he agreed. Glancing at the dark sky above them, he hoped it wouldn't be as bad the weatherman had forecast. "It's supposed to be a few inches."

Reaching the door to the office, he opened and held it for her, then followed her inside to the empty waiting area. "There's no one here," he observed, pointing at the glass cubical.

"There's no need for the receptionist," Dr. Melody Castleberry called from behind them, standing in the patient entrance to the back areas. "I'm only seeing three people today."

Above her teal colored mask, the greenest eyes he had ever seen sparkled at Ben. "Hello, I'm Benjamin Monroe," he stammered as he stepped forward and offered his hand. Instantly regretting the move, he withdrew the appendage. "Sorry, I forgot." Warm air escaped the edges of his mask as he breathed heavily behind it.

Grinning ear to ear, Candy's simple white cloth covered her pleasure at seeing him fumble for words. "I'll take it from here," she informed him as she weaved past the couple who stood frozen in the awkward introduction.

"It's nice to meet you," Melody informed him, her bright red locks shimmering when she shook them, sending fiery waves through the cascade of curls hanging down her back. "I'm going to take care of… my patient," she offered as she turned to the open portal. "You're welcome to wait here. No one else will be coming in until after lunch."

Following her, Ben's head filled with fog. Taking an empty chair next to the triage area, he watched as the doctor gathered Candy's weight and vitals. About five-foot-five, she was the perfect height for him, the top of her head reaching his nose. She had an average build, her lab coat hinted at her womanly curves.

Swallowing, he followed the process, taking in every detail of the woman behind those emerald-green eyes.

"We'll take room six," Dr. Castleberry directed, glancing at the man who had brought Candy to the office that morning. "Are you a friend of the family?" she asked while she waited for Candy to undress for her exam.

"You could say that." Ben laughed, adjusting his mask and resisting the urge to remove it. "I'm part of the bubble. I live in the house across the street, with Lanelle's nurse and the Ford family nanny slash housekeeper." He cut the air as he spoke, giving Caroline her dual role. "We do everything together these days." He felt silly, tongue-tied like a schoolboy.

"Well. We can't be too careful these days."

"No, we can't," he murmured as she turned and sauntered up to door number six. Knocking sharply with a bent knuckle, she waited for Candy's reply, then disappeared inside.

As soon as the door closed, Ben yanked the mask off his face and ran his hand wildly across his stubble. He hadn't even bothered to shave, knowing it wouldn't matter if he did. His heart pounding, he chastised himself for getting so worked up. "But damn, she's pretty," he mused aloud. *Well, from the nose up*. The idea of judging half a face brought on a fit of laugher, and he did his best to do so quietly. In the silence, he could hear music playing somewhere in the office, but not the typical canned elevator style. A real song sung by a performer, he hummed along with the happy tune.

Glancing at the closed door, he didn't even want to think about the exam taking place on the other side. Instead, he pondered what it would be like to date someone during a pandemic. "I mean, I can't just ask her out for coffee." That would never do. "We could Skype, maybe. Or Zoom. That's pretty popular these days." The sound of his voice as he talked to himself muffled the music, then a new song began, which played slightly louder.

Not needing to strain, Ben caught the words easily and began to sing along, forgetting to be quiet. A rich baritone, his voice echoed off the walls until he became aware of laugher from the tiny room the two women occupied. *Damn.* He was busted.

Pursing his lips, he covered his face with his mask. Sulking for a moment, he noticed the caddy of notepaper and pens on the nurse's station before him. "What the hell," he muttered as he stood, snatching a slip of paper and pen. "You only live once, right?" Scrawling his name and phone number across it, he returned the pen and reclaimed his seat to wait.

Fortunately, he didn't have to suffer long before the door opened and Candy emerged, her doctor close behind. He couldn't see the smile, but he knew it was there. "Ok, ok, so I enjoy good music," he defended before she could say a word.

"That's all right," Melody soothed, her voice noticeably light. "I'm glad you enjoyed it."

"I did," he clipped shortly, anxious over his next move. Offering the slip of paper, he waited for her to take it.

Seeing the gesture, Candy's heart thumped loudly in her ears as she made a break for the front door. Behind her, she could hear their muffled conversation as her doctor accepted the note, whatever it was. Waiting patiently for their departure, her mood had vastly improved over the course of their visit because of the good news she had received; there were no signs of eclampsia, and her pregnancy was progressing normally, so far. Or could it be her happiness for their dear friend, who had come to be a huge part of their lives?

"Thanks," Ben offered when he joined her, ready to guide her to his car.

"Don't mention it," she sang. Reaching the sedan, she climbed in, then observed, "So, may I inquire as to the note?"

"No, you may not," Ben toyed with her. "I wouldn't want to get any gossip started." *Or anyone's hopes up*, he added mentally.

"Well, she's a good age for you," Candy insisted, unable to stop herself from playing match maker, at least a little. There was a time she had thought Cathy might have been interested in Ben, but the age difference would have always been an issue. "Professional, too. Obviously."

"Yeah, I've met women before, Candice. I can handle it. If anything comes of it," he cocked his head towards her, teasing her, "you'll be the first to know."

FIVE

Let It Snow

DAKOTA AWOKE from his mid-day nap to bright white light. Flinging back his covers, he scampered over to his window and peered down at the front yard below. "Snow," he breathed, his warm air frosting the pane.

Making a mad dash for the door, he descended the stairs while calling "Snow! Snow!" at the top of his lungs.

"Yes, it's snow," Caroline chastised when he reached the kitchen. "Inside voice, please." Daks had been doing well with his manners, but there were times his excitement still got the better of him. Fortunately, Joylana had woken up first or she would really be angry.

In her highchair, Joy cackled and mimicked, "Snow." Adding a few loud whacks to the tabletop portion with her spoon, she joined in her brother's celebration.

"Outside," Daks announced. "Jo'ana go play?"

"Not right now," Carol countered with a giggle. "You need to eat, and you have to be dressed for outside play." Placing his sandwich on the table, she returned to tidying up the dishes.

Clambering into his chair, Daks wasted little time finishing the meal as there was a winter wonderland outside begging to be spoiled with footprints and snow mounds; he hadn't quite mastered the art of snowman building yet.

Peeking through the window in the back door, Holly shook her head. "I don't know. It's coming down pretty hard. This might not be a good time to be out in it."

"Nonsense," Lanelle slurred. Seated in her chair, she had been watching her grandchildren, as eager to be out of the house as they were.

"Now, Mimi," Holly soothed. "You know you don't want to catch a cold."

Lanelle only glared at her with piercing steel-blue eyes.

"Outside," Daks insisted, prompting Joy to bang more.

"All right, all right!" Carol shouted above the racket. "We'll try it for a few minutes, but everyone eats and dresses warmly, first." Catching her lover's eyes, she grinned. "It will be, you know . We won't let them stay out long."

But that did little for Holly. It was her job to worry. Lanelle's health was fragile at best, so allowing her to become chilled just wouldn't work for her. "I'll figure something out," she reluctantly agreed.

Half an hour later, the requisite demands had been met and Caroline prepared to lead their group out to the back yard. In her wheelchair, Lanelle had been dressed in a warm jacket for her arms and torso, while a thick wool blanket covered her legs. Beneath it, a hot-water bottle added an extra degree of warmth.

Opening the back door, Carol escorted the children out first. Little legs pumping, Joy did her best to keep up with her older brother, and peals of laughter soon echoed off the large trees that spotted their large back yard.

Getting her wheelchair out through the doorway, Holly parked Lanelle near the railing for the best view. "Can you see?"

"Yes," Lanelle rasped, drawing her jacket tighter around the neck. "Top half's cold."

Leaving her, Holly hurried back inside to retrieve another blanket. Dropping it over her charge's shoulders, she observed the sparkle in the older woman's eyes. Making one more trip, she located her own jacket and gloves.

"Where are you going?" Carol demanded when she returned donning the items.

"To play in the snow," Holly quipped. "Lanelle can't be out in it, but I can do it for her."

Carol beamed at her lover, accepting the caring gesture. "Go on, baby. I'll get anything she needs." She was fairly certain her partner's motives weren't purely altruistic as Holly darted into the drifts and began helping Daks pack snow onto his mound.

Almost an hour later, a dark sedan cleared the back of the house and pulled up at their garage that took up the back left of the property. "Mommy!" Daks sang out when she had climbed out of the car.

Seeing her mother, Joylana squealed and began the arduous trek across the growing piles of snow behind him.

"Oh, my babies," Candy exclaimed. Dropping to her knees, she hugged each in turn. Grasping at Joy's mitten covered fingers, she asked, "How long have they been outside?"

"About long enough," Carol called from the porch.

"Nooo," Daks resisted.

"I'm afraid so," Holly agreed, tromping over to help her employer coral the children. "We've been out at least forty-five minutes, and that's plenty cold at one time."

"That's long enough, baby," Candy soothed. Seeing her struggle, Ben used her left arm to help her to her feet.

"Let's go in and have a warm snack," he coaxed. "Momma and I need some lunch."

"They ate just a bit ago," Holly observed, "but it could be time for a snack after all our hard work," she added, indicating the large pile they had manage to scrape together.

Ben cocked an eyebrow at the sight. "What's that supposed to be."

"Snowman!" Daks informed him loudly, quite proud of their accomplishment.

"You bet it is," Candy added, scooping her daughter into her arms and adjusting her against her hip aside her round belly.

"You sure seem to be in a better mood," Carol observed when they reached the back porch.

"Yes," Candy replied airily as she climbed the steps. "The doctor visit was good news."

Holly cut her a sideways glance before she began the process of moving Lanelle back inside. "Were you expecting it not to be?" What good did it do to have a full-time nurse on the premises if she was not kept informed about things?

"Oh, I just worry," Candy replied flippantly, choosing not to spoil the rest of their day with her dark thoughts.

Removing their jackets and shaking off the snow, the small kitchen soon filled with the smell of grilled cheese, hot tomato soup, and whipped cream topped cocoa, along with the sounds of a happy winter's day in the Ford family bubble.

"Well, the steaks smell delicious," Holly offered as the group gathered around the larger dining room table.

"Indeed," Roger confirmed, having had a hand in their preparation.

His co-chef, Ben only laughed, anxiously keeping

an eye on his morning charge. Seated next to Gary's empty setting, Candy rubbed her belly, obviously distracted. "Are you going to eat now or wait for the big man?" he teased.

"For what?" Candice only half joined them, her mind still somewhere else.

"For Gary, your husband," Benjamin enunciated more clearly. Taking the seat across from her, with the vacant head of the table between them, he said more gently. "I'm sure he's fine. He'll be home as soon as he is able."

Her eyes flicking to the darkness beyond the window, she longed to see headlights turning into the drive. "He should have been here hours ago. He said he would be here in time for dinner, didn't he Carol?"

"That was my impression," the housekeeper agreed. Spooning mashed potatoes onto a plate for Joylana, she hesitated, unsure how to comfort their lady of the house.

"He's a grown man, Candy. Something came up. He wasn't able to call, or he would have; and that's that." Roger's firm tone brought down the noise of the group for a moment as they considered his stern observation.

Lights glided across the wall and Candy ignored the rebuke. Getting to her feet, she balanced herself against the table before mumbling a reply and departing for the kitchen. Reaching the back door, she pulled back the curtain and watched Gary's suburban slowly ease into the garage. "Damn him," she whispered hoarsely.

Reaching the back door, Gerald opened it gently, noting the darkness of the room as he entered. Before he called out, Candy stepped forward, the light from the living area illuminating her shorter frame.

"Where were you?" Her voice shrill, she fought to prevent it from reaching the diners down the hall.

"We had an emergency," he stated flatly, closing the portal and reaching for her. Lifting her slightly, he squeezed. "Awe, Kitten, I'm so sorry."

"You should have been here hours ago." She wept against the cool leather of his jacket. Smelling the shampoo fresh in his damp hair, she whispered, "You've been to a fire."

"Yes," he confessed, his cheek pressed against the top of her head. "I don't want to worry you, baby."

"You did worry me," she spat, fighting to extricate herself from his grasp.

Allowing her a little room, he whispered, "Can we talk about this later? I assume from your demeanor and the noise in the other room I haven't totally missed dinner."

"No, you haven't missed it," she sniveled, wiping at her tears. "My god, Gary, why didn't you call?"

"I didn't have time. Things happened so fast, once I had time in the truck…well, you know how noisy that is. You wouldn't have been able to hear a word I said," he joked, hoping to calm her.

Looking up at him, the light from the other room lit up his face just enough to see his drawn features. "You don't want to tell me."

"No," he agreed, shaking his head slowly. "We'll

talk tonight, once everyone is gone. I'm not hiding it from you, Kitten. I would just rather it be between us."

"All right," she relented, her hands massaging the arms that still half held her. Painting a smile on her face, she marched back to the group to serve their plates.

"Where's Gary?" Eve demanded, as if her daughter-in-law had hidden him somewhere.

"He's taking off his coat." Candy sniffed, fighting to maintain her composure. "He had to go on a call."

"A call," Roger spat, turning to his son as he entered the room. "I thought you were taking a leave of absence."

Reaching his seat, Gary rested his hands on the highbacked chair. Inhaling deeply, he released the air in a slow gush. "I was hoping to avoid this conversation," he confessed.

"What, are you not taking leave?" Eve spat.

"I'm taking it, just not now," Gary replied calmly. Pulling out the seat, he sat down and picked at his plate. "Thank you, Kitten. This looks delicious."

Most of the others had finished their meal and simply sat staring from their end of table, waiting for the couple to explain the situation they all shared a stake in. Seeing that they would not be satisfied until he had divulged the day's events, Gary offered his palms and shrugged. "Fine, I'll explain. But I imagine no one here is going to be happy about what I have to say."

SIX

Darkness Falls

"I WASN'T GOING to tell any of the rest of you," Gary explained. "I decided that on the way home. You are much happier not knowing."

"Just spill it already, son," Roger half joked, his straight face making his words hard to read. "The suspense if killing us."

"Well, when I got to Fred Johnson's office, things were a little hectic," Gary began, "so, I had to wait. The vaccine approval came at the end of last week, and they are dealing with that among all the normal day-to-day down at the central offices for emergency services."

"We do watch the news," Eve sniffed. "We are aware this will all soon be over."

Holly stiffened in her seat next to Carol, who reached beneath the table and took her hand. Giving it a squeeze, she ensured the nurse would hold her opinions if she could help it.

"The vaccine will be distributed, but this is far

from over," Gary stated succinctly. "In fact, it is likely to get much worse before it gets better." Cutting his eyes around at the group, some only friends but all were considered family, his voice deepened. "I'm thankful each and every one of you is here. We are going to make it through whatever comes."

"Gary, you're scaring me," Candy whispered, resting her fork against her plate.

"I'm sorry, Love," he replied. Leaning back in his chair, he ran his hand through his hair. "One of the houses, number twenty-two, has been shut down. Well, their crew have all been placed on leave. We had to pull men from everywhere else to fill the roster, so I can't take my leave right now."

Instantly, ragged breaths wracked Candy's body. She didn't know how much having him home would mean to her until that moment. She wailed behind her hands as she pressed them to her face, wishing with her entire being she had heard this news in private.

"I'm sorry, Kitten," Gary soothed, leaning forward to run a large hand up and down her curved back as she hunched over her swollen belly. "I'll get the leave as soon as I'm able."

"You're going to miss him being born," she moaned.

"Maybe not. Look, Baby, this is bigger than us. I know this is important but people are sick. People are dying."

"You're a fireman," Eve interrupted. "You have the means to quit that job and I suggest that you do so. Your family needs you."

"A lot of people need me right now, Mother," Gary insisted. "I'm sure my family understands. This is something I have to do." Cutting his eyes over at her, he dared her to say anything else with his glare.

Picking up on the chill, Holly cleared her throat. "Well, since we are on the subject of being needed, I also have something to share." She sat up straighter in her chair as all eyes turned to her. "The hospice center I worked for before I came here has reached out to me."

"Hospice," Lanelle uttered.

"Not about you, Love," Holly clarified. "You are doing fine. This is also something beyond our little group. I'm sure you are all aware of the hospital situation. They are full and overflowing across the state, and even the country." She paused, anxiously taking in each face. "There is an acute shortage of nurses," she finished flatly.

"You wouldn't leave us," Candy shrieked. Could this day get any worse? "I knew the other shoe was going to drop!"

"Oh, Baby," Gary chuckled at her drama. Leaning over, he pulled her into a hug. "I'm sure our Holly wouldn't abandon your mother, or all of us, at a time like this."

"Well, that's the thing," Holly near whispered. "I'm not leaving, but I am seriously considering going to help."

"You're going to work at the hospital?" Roger gasped. "Wasn't this supposed to be a bubble away from all that risk?" He indicated his son at the opposite end of the table. "It's bad enough Gary is out in it, and now you want to go work in the thick of it?" His voice had risen as he spoke, growing uncustomarily loud.

"No, Grampa," Holly insisted. "I'm not going to be at the hospital. They have put together a mobile unit to help distribute the vaccine, but they need qualified people to run it," she calmly explained, her mind made up on the issue. All she had to do was sell the others. "They are starting with the nursing homes, and they will need nurses who can help with the administration. It's quite involved. Not just anyone can volunteer," she finished, her voice trailing away.

Silence fell over the room, everyone either too stunned or too concerned to speak. Squeezing the digits she still held, Caroline said gently, "You didn't tell me you were considering this."

"I wasn't," Holly stammered, meeting her gaze. "I just got the call today. I hadn't even thought about it until they sought me out."

"Why you?" Gary prodded; suspicious it would happen on this day by chance.

"I'm sure it's not just me," she replied airily. "I'm registered, that's all. I'm sure they are contacting everyone they can think of to help with the vaccination campaign. It will be massive and will require trained nurses, who are in short supply."

The sound of Candy fighting hysteria surrounded them, her ragged breathing becoming controlled. "You'll take precautions," she managed. "Both of you will be careful not to bring the virus here. Or to become infected."

Gary shrugged. "My exposure is still low."

"Mine will be as well," Holly defended.

"How did twenty-two become quarantined, then?" Ben asked innocently, having stayed out of the conversation until then.

"Someone brought it in," Gary confessed. "One of the guys. He was exposed and apparently asymptomatic. Unfortunately, it spread in the house and now the whole team is down."

"How long?" Candy whispered, her mind clearing. "Our little Gary is due Christmas day."

"Two weeks," Gary clipped, sad at sharing the news. "Maybe it will end sooner, though. Or maybe he'll come late." He laughed loudly, hoping that would be the case. Otherwise, he really was going to miss it, more than likely.

SEVEN

In the Shadow

TWO DAYS LATER, Gary spent the night at the station, leaving Candy all alone in their giant bed. Twisting and turning in the darkness, she did her best to get some sleep. "Eight days," she mumbled to herself periodically. Scowling at the ceiling above her, she thought about their wedding anniversary, which fell on Christmas Eve. If this night were any indication, she would spend it alone.

Her mind turning, it occurred to her that she might start their next year together in the hospital, having given birth to their third child. Caressing where his foot dug into her ribs, she smiled despite the discomfort. "This holiday is getting very crowded," she informed him. They would have to be extra diligent to ensure their son still had a special day in the years to come, or he might get lost amongst all the chaos this time of year always brought her.

Deciding sleep wasn't going to be her friend, Candy threw back the covers and put her stocking feet on the bare floor. She had told Gary she liked the hardwood surfaces throughout the house, but the cold flat surface chilling her toes as she moved to get dressed might have changed her mind.

Rummaging in a drawer for something warm, she happened upon her running suit. "Gosh I haven't been for a morning jog in ages," she quietly mused, aware that Melody Castleberry had advised against it once she started her third trimester. "She didn't forbid walking, though." Digging underneath it, she found one that would fit her rounder form. Moving quickly to don the outfit in the chill air, she traced the line of her full belly in front of the mirror when she was done.

"Well, you'll be here soon," she informed him, patting her son gently through her abdominal wall.

Picking up her shoes, she slipped through the bathroom to the nursery. Joylana still slept there, but they planned to move her over the weekend. Her bedroom had been set up in Carol's old room, and she played in it every day. They hoped it would get her used to the space before the transition became permanent.

Running a curved finger along a pudgy cheek, Candy traced the line of her daughter's dark ringlets. Her deep ebony skin blended with the shadows of the dimly lit room, bringing a smile to her lips. "My sweet girl," she whispered.

They had adopted Joy back when she was too afraid to try for a child of their own. Heck, she still feared what might happen in the days to come, but with only a week or so left in her pregnancy, she had to admit it appeared everything would turn out fine with the birth of their son. Of course, that made having Joylana in their family even more special, and her uniqueness blended perfectly in their home where everyone was so different. "I love you, little girl," she whispered before she slipped from the room.

Downstairs, she crept into the kitchen, noting the soft glow of light from her mother's room. "Are you awake?" she hissed.

"It's me," Holly informed her, presenting herself in the doorway. "Lanelle had a slight cough before I left last night, and I wanted to evaluate her early in morning."

"And?" Candy prodded, gripping her Nikes tight enough to turn her knuckles white.

"She sounds good," Holly supplied, pulling the door and switching on the kitchen light. "Are you going for a run?"

"A walk, actually. I didn't sleep well with Gary gone. I'm hoping it will calm me."

"You might be nesting," Holly observed gently. "Would you like a hot apple cider? Maybe a little coffee when you get back?" She pulled out the pot and began to prepare their morning brew.

"I'd love it," Candice agreed, a sense of relief washing over her. "I won't be long. Daks and Joy are still asleep."

"Oh, they'll be fine. Carol was in the shower when I left. She's anxious to get to the grocery while it's quiet and I told her I could hold things down here."

"Good, then I'll go have my walk and warm up with a spot of coffee when I get back," Candy agreed as she tied her shoes.

Leaving by the back door, Candy watched her footing as she took the ramp they had added for Lanelle's wheelchair. Reaching the ground, she found it firm, as most of the snow had melted after the brief coating from the other day. Making it to the sidewalk next to the street, she relaxed, swinging her arms as she walked at a brisk pace.

It felt good to get her heartrate up, and she briefly pondered why she hadn't done it before. "Exercise has always lifted my spirits," she said to herself. When she arrived back at the house, almost an hour had passed.

"I'm sorry I was gone so long," she apologized as she removed her brightly colored mittens and hat.

"It's all right," Lanelle slurred from her favorite chair at the table. "Sometimes you have to take care of you."

Holly grinned at the older woman as she placed a warm cup on the table for Candy, then served one for herself. "You are right on time," she stated firmly. "The kids aren't even awake yet."

"That's a relief," Candy murmured, clasping the warm mug. "It felt so good, I had to drag myself back here."

"How's the baby?" Holly asked casually.

"Behaving himself, actually," Candy informed her

with a light laugh. "He's calmed down a lot these last few days. A lot less kicking, unless I'm trying to sleep." Glancing at her mother, her smile lessened, she added, "This is much different than when Dakota was born." Back then, she had hidden her pregnancy, which had nearly cost them both their lives.

"It's ok," Lanelle lamented, following her daughter's thoughts. "Enjoy your new baby."

Wishing to change the subject, Candy studied their nurse. "Have you accepted the position with the vax-mobile yet?"

"Yes." Holly nodded. "I completed all my paperwork yesterday. I go tomorrow for a walkthrough and training session and will be a part of the team starting next week." Catching herself, she added, "Of course, I told them I would not be available as much once the baby comes. I'll need to be here at least for a few weeks."

"We'll be fine," Lanelle interjected, grinning at her daughter. "She's a good momma and I don't need much."

Candy lost a bit of her enthusiasm. "It would have really helped if Gary could have gotten the leave of absence."

"Yes, but we can't help that, now can we?" Holly countered, hoping to keep her employer from slipping any further down. "Don't let it bother you, Candy. We'll get through this."

"I'm not," Candy agreed, inhaling deeply, then pushing down on the top of her belly. "Tell me again how you know you won't become infected."

"Well," Holly replied with a grin. "I will wear my mask. And the patients who come for their vaccine will also wear their masks. Together, that alone will reduce the chances of getting infected. Plus, they are going to vaccinate me tomorrow when I do my training. It will take a few weeks to kick in, but after that I won't be able to catch the virus. As long as I wash and disinfect on top of that, you guys will be safe until it's your turn." Seeing the pensive expression form on her employer's features, she added, "Don't worry. I wouldn't do it if I weren't confident of your safety."

Candy nodded thoughtfully. She had been mulling over what she knew and had decided that Gary and Holly were both right. Their family needed them, but so did their community. They had been hiding in their little bubble for three quarters of a year; they were safe enough. It would be asking too much to demand the two of them not help. "I understand. We can't hide in the shadow of fear."

At that moment, the back door opened, and Gary clomped his way inside. "Good morning everyone," he sang, not really having expected to see them all sitting there when he entered.

Standing, Candy waited for him to remove his coat and boots, then presented herself for a welcoming cuddle. "I missed you last night," she cooed.

"I guess I'm forgiven, then," he whispered into her hair as he hugged her.

"Indeed, you are." Stepping back, she grinned.

"I've just been for a walk and I need to put a load of laundry in the wash. Are you going to bed?"

"Laundry," Gary repeated with surprise. Pouring a cup of coffee, he looked around. "Where's Carol?"

"Shopping," all three women said in unison.

"Oh," he replied, taking a noisy sip and wondering if there were more to it than that. Deciding to let it go, he said instead, "I'm going to take a nap, but not a long one. I got some sleep at the station last night and I don't need much."

"All right, then maybe we can finish moving Joylana to her new room," Candy suggested.

"Sounds good," Gary agreed, again surprised by his wife's demeanor. Watching her as she exited the room and took to the stairs, he mused, "Well, she's full of energy today."

"She's nesting," Holly informed him. "You should push them about that leave."

"What's nesting?" he asked, ignoring the issue that could not be resolved, at least not right then.

"It happens when the baby engages in the birth canal. The head drops down and the uterus hangs lower in the body, relieving some of the pressure on the lungs and other organs. The mother feels better and many are not even be aware of why."

"I see," Gary mused, holding his mug in front of his face. "Does it last long?"

"It means she will likely give birth soon. You may not have until Christmas," Holly informed him gently.

"Oh," Gary coughed. Glancing at his mother-in-law, he swallowed, then placed his cup in the sink.

"I've changed my mind on that nap. I need to make a phone call." Leaving them, he went to his office and closed the door.

Taking out his phone, Gary made a call, then listened to it ring.

"Hello?" A deep voice greeted from the other end.

"Hey, Mac. It's Gerald Ford. Remember that favor I had asked you about?"

"Yes, sir." James Macdonald had not had much in the way of business for months; of course, he remembered.

"I think I'm ready to collect," Gary informed him with a grin.

"Sounds good," Mac confirmed. "Load her up and bring her down, and we'll get started right away."

Shoving his phone into his rear pocket, Gary contemplated how to make his move. He did want this to be a surprise after all, which meant he needed to be a bit deceptive.

Returning to the kitchen, he prepared his tale. "Lanelle, I need you to go shopping with me," he began. Holly and Lanelle turned to look at him in unison. "I've got something special picked out for Candy and I need your opinion on it," he tried again.

Lanelle grinned. "You's always a sweetheart, Gerald Ford. Help me dress, Holly."

"You want me to accompany you?" Their nurse felt surprised by the sudden shopping spree and hadn't planned on taking Lanelle anywhere until she had been vaccinated.

"No, the two of us can handle it," Gary informed her, giving his mother-in-law a wink.

Helping Lanelle into her room, they were dressing her when Candy came down carrying her basket of laundry.

"You need any help with that on the stairs?" Gary offered as he waited.

"I can manage," his wife replied cheerily as she switched on the basement light, then closed the door behind her as she disappeared into her chore.

"Are you about ready in there?" he demanded through Lanelle's closed portal. "I want to be gone before Candy gets back up here."

"In fact, we are," Holly sang, swinging back the plank of wood, but still not certain about the outing. "Mind if I ask where you are taking her?"

"She'll be safe," he informed their nurse with a half grin, proud of how protective she was. Grasping the handles on her wheelchair, he gave a hefty push to get Lanelle out the back door. "Tell Candy we are both taking a nap if she asks," he instructed on the way out, gently closing the exit behind him.

EIGHT

Secrets and Surprises

BALANCING her basket on her belly with one hand, Candy trailed the other along the rough wooden banister. Taking it slow, she exhaled loudly when she reached the bottom. "Boy, that was exciting," she said to the empty space. She could not remember the last time she did laundry for herself or even came to the basement.

Glancing around, she moved to the washer and set up her load. Deciding to do a load of lights and another of darks, she quickly sorted the clothing on the large table that occupied the center of the room. While she worked, she thought about how school had gone that semester. She had deeply dreaded it back before the fall, but now that it had ended, she felt an overpowering sense of relief. She caressed her belly. "I may be able to finish this next year if all goes well."

Running her hand over her belly, she could say

the same thing about her pregnancy. She had been terrified upon hearing the news, but now—with the end in sight—she found herself enjoying the experience and was certainly happy to have been blessed. "And Christmas hasn't been bad either, all things considered."

Looking up at the ceiling above her and picturing their living room above her head, she recalled the day their tree had been delivered. Roger and Eve had come to help with the decorating in a new and wonderful tradition she hoped would endure even after the bubble lost its usefulness. They still waited on a few packages that hadn't arrived, but for the most part the approaching holiday seemed the brightest she could recall.

Deciding to get the load that had begun to agitate into the dryer before she went back upstairs, she wandered around the dimly lit room. Shelves lined the walls, where Gary stored all sorts of man things. Noticing a few of them had been covered with old sheets, presumably to keep the dust off, she grew curious at what he might be hiding from her.

Peeking beneath one end, a lump formed in her gut at the stack of canned goods underneath. Lifting the material higher, gravity took over and it slid off, forming a heap on the floor in front of the rows of cans. And not just a few cans. Her fingers trembling, Candy reached for one, inspecting it. A simple can of fruit, the word PEACHES and a date had been inscribed on the top end. "What the hell?" she muttered out loud.

"You weren't supposed to find them."

Her pulse gushing in her ears, Candy turned to face their housekeeper. "What is this, Caroline?"

"It's a bit of food," Carol stated calmly. Stepping forward, into the light, she placed a pair of plastic bags on the plain wooden table. In her right hand, she fidgeted with a black marker.

"It's more than a bit," Candy shot back, horrified at the volume of containers. "We couldn't possibly eat all this!"

"It's just a…precaution. Something to fall back on if we need it," Carol defended.

"And what's this?" Candy pushed, showing her the end of the can.

"In case we lose the label," Carol whispered. "Please, Candy. Don't be mad."

"I'm not mad," her employer spat. "Honestly. I don't understand." She waved a hand, indicating the wall of shelves. Catching more of the coverings, she pulled at them, causing the pile on the floor to grow. "Why would you do this?"

"Because it made me feel better." Carol sniffed, her voice thick with sadness. "When the pandemic first started, the shelves were so empty. We had to scrounge to get what we needed."

"I remember."

"Yes," Carol agreed, taking a few steps closer. Grasping her arm, she gave her friend a squeeze. "It really scared me that we might not have enough to feed all of us. And then the bubble kept growing. Ben came, then Eve and Roger."

"You were worried about us?" Such a thing had never occurred to her, and they certainly had never talked about it. "Carol, I find this a bit irrational."

"Not to me," Caroline defended. If things got hard, they would need every bit of that food. "Are you going to tell Gary?" she inquired meekly.

"He doesn't know?" Candy asked in surprise. "How did you buy all this?"

"I just added it to the weekly grocery bill. A bit at a time, I bought things that would be safe to eat, even if it were years from now."

"And you hid them in our basement," Candy stated incredulously. "I'm really confused, here," she confessed. Stacking the can back with the others, she looked past their lanky nanny and glared at the fresh bags. "Every week?"

"Every week," Carol echoed, lifting her chin.

"We have to tell Gary," Candy informed her. "I'm not prepared to keep a secret like this from him." Taking a step back, she surveyed the silver tower. What the hell were they going to do with all of it?

At that moment, the washer spun to a stop. On instinct, Carol turned to move the articles over to the dryer. "Please don't be mad," she whispered when Candy joined her. "I just felt better. Like I was in control somehow. Like we were safer. And then I couldn't stop. Every time I go to the grocery, there are shelves that are bare, and I just want to put back more."

"Is this all of it?" Candy asked gently as she put her second load in the wash, terrified of answer.

"I've got some extra toilet paper under the sinks," Carol confessed with a short laugh. "We certainly didn't want to run out of that."

Candy grinned at the thought of it. "I can't fault you for that. Don't worry. We'll talk to Gary and see what he thinks about it. Who knows?" She shrugged, pausing to contemplate the conversation. "Maybe he'll agree with you."

"Or maybe he'll throw a tantrum and come down on me for wasting grocery money," Carol countered, hanging her head.

"I doubt it. He's probably the most even-tempered person I have ever met," Candy stated firmly. Indicating the bags, she suggested, "Let's go up for a hot drink while the laundry runs, and we can decide exactly how we are going to break this to him."

Riding next to Gary in his old suburban, Lanelle watched the passing buildings in silence. Her trips out of the house had become nearly nonexistent over the year, so little had changed for her when the pandemic started. However, she could see the effect it had had on everyone else.

Mask-covered faces along the sidewalk kept their distance from each other. Several buildings were boarded up, and too many were closed to indicate Christmas loomed only a week away. "So sad," she murmured.

"Yes, things have been rough," Gary agreed. "I hope we can recover."

"We have to recover," Lanelle lamented.

Pulling up in front of a glass store front, he parked the vehicle and leapt out to pull her chair from the back. Helping her out of the car seat and into the wheelchair, Gary took his time and handled her gently. "How's that?" he asked once she was settled.

"Feels good," Lanelle agreed with a toothy grin. She had always liked her son-in-law and the way he cared for everyone in his charge. Eyeing the front of the medical supply, she wondered what they could be doing there.

Pushing her inside, Gary grinned from ear to ear. "Hello, Mac!"

"Gary." The shopkeeper gave him a nod, then turned to his patron. "So, we are going to fashion you a new chair, are we?"

"Are we?" Lanelle gasped, not sure what to make of the suggestion. "I have a chair."

"We are getting you a better chair," Gary informed her, kneeling beside her. "This one is clunky and has to be pushed."

Lanelle stared at him, processing his words. "Yes."

"I want to buy a motorized chair." He used his hand with dangling fingers to simulate walking back and forth. "You can go across to the girl's and back to our house without help."

Her eyes widened. "You want me to drive myself?"

"Yeah," Gary agreed, his eyes misty. "I know this means admitting you will always need the chair." They had hoped at some point she would recover and regain her mobility, but after a year of pushing he around, it was time to face reality. "Lanelle, you are too young to depend on one of us to take you where you want to go. You need a bit of freedom." He grinned at her, waiting for her reply.

Her bright blue eyes staring into his, Lanelle sat in silence for a full minute.

"Don't be afraid," he comforted, placing his large hand over hers and giving it a squeeze. "Mac here is going to get you fitted for one that will be comfortable and easy to handle."

"Will it go fast?" Her voice quavered.

"Well, not if you don't want it to," he soothed.

Cutting her eyes up at the clerk, Lanelle grinned. "I want it to go real fast."

Both men burst into laughter. Gary had warned James that she might be a hard sell on the idea of having a permanent chair, but it appeared she would be a soft sell after all. "Let's get you up so I can get some measurements," he suggested.

They spent the rest of the morning poking, prodding, and picking out features. Every time she would say something was too expensive to add, Gary would insist they must have it. "This chair will add life to your years," he said more than once when she became obstinate.

By lunch, they had the perfect device planned, each of them thrilled with the work they had done by the time they loaded her back into the suburban. "If all goes well, we'll be able to pick it up before Christmas," Gary informed her as they belted her in.

"It would be nice." Lanelle beamed, happy that her family loved her so much.

NINE

Confront and Confess

"VROOM," Daks called loudly, his toy car skidding across the hardwood floor.

"Vrm vrm," Joy echoed, dragging the large red firetruck behind him.

Candy giggled at the pair, thinking they probably should trade, as the old truck Gary had bought the year they met was a bit much for her daughter's small frame. Managing to get down on the floor next to them, she asked, "Hey Daks. What if Santa brought you new woowoos this year? Would you like that?"

Halting in his tracks, the boy stared at her. Abandoning the engine, Joy scampered to her mother's side and pushed for a seat on her crowded lap. "Woowoos," she repeated happily, her own pink firetruck one of her favorite toys.

Taking her small dark hand, Candy caressed her fingers, then splayed them against her belly. "Can you feel him moving?" she asked quietly.

Joy grinned, "Baby."

"Yes, our baby is in mommy's tummy. Soon he's going to come out!" The back door opened, interrupting their play. "Ugh. Now I have to get up," Candy teased. Displacing the two-year-old, she rolled onto her knees and used the edge of the couch to make it to her feet as her husband wheeled her mother into the room. "I thought you two were taking a nap!" she confronted once she could face them squarely.

"Our cover is blown," Gary teased. "If I had known how long we would be gone, I would have thought of a better excuse."

Not saying a word, Lanelle beamed up at her daughter, only drawing more suspicion. "Mom?" Candy demanded. "You aren't going to tell me where you went?"

"Nope." Lanelle shook her head slowly. Gary had sworn her to secrecy, and the family would just have to wait until the chair was ready to find out the surprise.

"Fine," Candy grumbled, only half pretending to be put out. "Gary, Carol needs to speak with you," she informed him quietly. In the kitchen, the housekeeper prepared their lunch in silence, her own brand of sulking.

"What's going on?" Gary asked as he followed his wife into the other room.

"I'll let her tell you," Candy advised, folding her arms across her chest, then resting them on her round belly.

Sighing loudly, Caroline selected a towel to wipe her hands, then slowly turned to face them. "It might be better if I showed him. I don't really know how to explain it."

"Fine, let's go downstairs," Candy suggested. Stomping over to the door, she flung it open and flicked on the light. Leading the way, they followed her down at her slower pace. When they reached the bottom, she moved into the room and stood still, patiently waiting for her husband to notice.

"Ok, what am I supposed to see?" Gary asked. His eyes darting around, he expected a flood, fire, or that some other drastic event had occurred.

Palms up, Candy indicating the wall of shelves. "Carol's been hoarding food," she announced.

Her lip curling as if she might cry, Caroline sniffled. "I'm sorry, Gary."

Turning slowly to face the tower of metal, Gary gasped, "But why?"

"I don't know why," Caroline confessed. "I just felt like we needed to have a little back up."

"This isn't a little backup," Gary sputtered. "No wonder our food costs have gone up. I thought it was rising prices, or even extra mouths." He shifted his gaze to their housekeeper. "I never imagined it was anything like this."

Caroline almost wished he would yell at her. That would have been far easier to take than the disappointed glare. "I'm sorry, Gary."

"Well, what's done is done," he countered, placing his hands on his hips and resuming studying the labels.

"The real question is what we are going to do with all of it," Candy observed.

"Well, some of it can stay, I guess," Gary suggested. "We might need a bit of back up some time with the way things are going. But most of it will need to go somewhere it can be used." He rubbed his chin roughly, then snapped his fingers. "I'll make a phone call."

Leaving the two girls in the cellar, Gary went to his office and made three calls in total before he returned. As soon as his footsteps creaked on the stairs the girls got quiet and waited for the verdict.

"Carol, Ben is going to come and help you box it up. You can keep fifty cans of whatever you like, but the rest needs boxed and hauled up to the back porch. I can help load it from there, probably in a few days. For now, I'm going to have lunch and take that nap I meant to have," he informed them sternly.

"Are you mad?" Candy asked as Carol scooted up the stairs to finish lunch.

"No, Kitten, I'm not mad." Gary shook his head as he chuckled, surveying the cans once more. "I guess I should have asked when the charges on the card started to climb."

Slipping beneath his arm, Candy leaned against him. "I think it made her feel safe," she explained. "She said all the empty shelves at the grocery were freaking her out about not having enough."

"Well, that's understandable," Gary lamented, "but there's only so much one family needs."

"Are you going to tell me what you and mom were up to today?"

"No." He laughed loudly, hugging her tightly with her belly between them. "It's a surprise, Kitten. But don't worry, I think you are going to like it."

TEN

House of Plenty

"MAN, THESE BOXES ARE GETTING HEAVY," Ben moaned as he stacked another in the back of the suburban.

"Tell me about it," Gary agreed, shuffling those in the third row of seats to fit a few in the cramped space. Leaving his friend to continue the packing, he went inside and brought out Lanelle, then pushed her chair down the ramp. Lifting her into the passenger seat, he asked quietly, "Are you excited?"

"Yes," Lanelle replied with a nod, eager to have her surprise.

Buckling her in, Gary sauntered around to the driver's side and started the engine to warm the compartment. "We'll be ready to leave in a few minutes," he informed her, then closed the door with a firm slam. "Are you girls ready?" he hollered towards the house before he resumed helping load the boxes of food.

"We're ready," Candy replied from the steps.

Gripping the railing, she made it to the bottom without losing her footing. "It's icy today. Are you sure we should be getting out?"

"I won't have another day off until Christmas," he gently reminded her. "So yeah, it will have to be today. Don't worry, I'll take it slow and easy."

Hoisting herself into the empty passenger seat, Carol sat behind Gary and Candy behind her mother. Adjusting into the cushioned chair, Candy glanced at the pile of boxes behind them, noting her mother's chair had been wedged in as well. "Good luck getting that out," she mumbled.

"We're dropping off the boxes first," Gary replied as he climbed behind the wheel. Easing out of the drive, Gary tested the slippery feel of the heavy load. Taking it slow and easy, as promised, they soon arrived in front of a large gray building.

"Catholic Charities," Candice breathed against her glass, studying the structure. How many times had they been to that very location when she and her mother needed a helping hand? She couldn't have counted them all if she had tried. "I haven't been here I in a long time," she observed. Not since she had met Gerald Ford, and her life had changed forever.

"They have the orphanage and run the food pantry," Gary clarified, grinning at his wife. "We have plenty at our house, and it won't hurt us to share with those who don't."

"Amen," Caroline whispered, happy her blunder would serve others in the end.

Climbing out and donning his mask, Gary left the

heater running while he went inside to announce their arrival and a few young men with wheeled carts came out to help unload the haul. Playing it off as if their donation was intentional, Gary made sure they had it all, then waved to one of the priests he had been talking to as he resumed his seat behind the wheel. Leaning across Lanelle's lap, he shoved a slip of paper into the glove box and slammed it shut.

"What's that?" Candy asked curiously.

"We donated so much, they gave us a receipt for our taxes." Pausing, he began to laugh. "I didn't have the heart to tell them why we were giving it all away."

Carol giggled as well. "Thank you, Gerald. I hate to admit it, but I am a little embarrassed. I mean, I knew my stockpile was growing, but I didn't realize there was anything wrong with it until I saw you guys' faces when you looked at it."

"It was quite a haul," Gary agreed, still chuckling. "Maybe next year we can do it again."

Candy barked out a laugh then, and all four enjoyed the happy moment until they turned the corner. Along the side of the building a line of masked people stretched, six-foot gaps spacing them apart. Rolling beside them, their mood darkened. When they reached the stop sign, Gary continued on straight, while the girls turned in their seats to observe those who waited ran the other side of the building as well.

"Did you give them any cash?" Candy's voice quavered.

"Yes, Kitten, I made a cash donation as well." Viewing her reflection in his mirror, he could see the lines drawn around her eyes. "We did a good thing today."

The drive to the medical supply somber, Lanelle seemed less excited about her new chair, that is until she saw it. Then, she bounced with glee, eager to climb into it and take it for a spin.

"You bought her a chair?" Candy demanded once they were inside, her tone sharp despite the cloth covering her mouth and nose.

"She's going to love it," Gary countered, offering his hand to Mac before he dropped it. "Dammit. I keep forgetting."

Mac pointed at his face. "You'd think the masks would remind you."

"Yes, but I'm so used to them, I don't even notice any more," Gary agreed. "Do you want to show her how it all works?"

"Of course." Mac opened a palm towards the device and Gary helped his mother-in-law into the new seat.

Standing back, Candy and Carol quietly observed the process, commenting to each other in whispers from time to time. When Lanelle finally had the hang of it, Candy gasped, "Not so fast, Mom!"

"She wanted the high-speed version," Mac informed her as he joined them.

"You're kidding me!" Candy squealed. "Gary, you didn't even ask me about this!"

"Meh." He shrugged. "I generally beg forgiveness. Asking permission means you can say no." He cut his eyes over at her and laughed at her squinted gaze. "She's going to be fine, Kitten. And this way, she can go over to see the girls, or even go around the block, if she wants to. She needs her independence."

"I guess," Candy mumbled, her mind still racing. "It could be dangerous, that's all."

"She can't live the rest of her life in three little rooms," Gary insisted more firmly.

Sensing a fight might be brewing, Caroline inched away, feigning interest in some of the displays. As if to agree, Mac also wandered away, leaving the couple alone.

"You could have asked or at least mentioned it," Candy snapped.

"That's not what you're mad about."

Gary's calmness irked her even more. "What's that supposed to mean?" Little Gary kicked hard, and her belly grew taut, causing her to wince as she said it. Gritting her teeth, she waited for the pain to pass.

"Are you all right , love?"

"I'm fine," she bit angrily. "Don't change the subject."

Sighing loudly, Gary let it go. "You're upset because this chair makes it permanent. Your mother will never be what she was. She is never going to get better."

"Pfft," she spat.

"It's ok. She can still enjoy the life she has. She has a lot of good years left, and we should all make the best of them."

Candy began to cry uncontrollably. Catching her, Gary pulled her into a firm embrace. "Let it out, Kitten," he soothed. "I knew this was going to be hard. That's why I didn't tell you." Pivoting, he pointed, "See how happy she is?"

Candy squinted to see her mother learning to steer, the grin on her mother's face undeniable. "You always hand out happy, don't you, Gerald Ford," she accused. "Like you're Santa Clause or something."

"I guess I do," he agreed, giving her a squeeze. "It makes me feel good when I do for others."

Leaning into him, she slid her arms around to return the hug the best she could. "A few more days and our baby boy will be here. Our little Gary," she observed with a sigh.

"Yeah, our little guy," he agreed, still watching the older woman's glee. "Are you really ok?"

"I'm fine. I'm just tired, and I hurt in places like I never have before. Not to sound bitter, but I'm really ready for the big debut."

"It can wait. Two more days and I'll be off from Christmas to New Year's day, even if I can't take an actual leave. Think you can hang on until then?"

"I'm not sure that it's up to me," she replied, rocking gently in the strength of her husband's arms. "But I'll give it my best," she agreed as her mother rode their way, obviously ready to take her new toy home.

ELEVEN

Ring the Bells

"HERE YOU GO, KITTEN." Gary offered his bride a cup of hot apple cider, taking a seat on the ottoman after she accepted it. Across from him, curled on one end of their sofa, she sipped noisily. "I wish I could stay home," he lamented quietly.

"No, no, baby. Your last shift before the holiday. We can make it." She watched him over the rim of her steaming mug. "I'm sure I'm just tired."

"You've been going pretty hard this past week," he solemnly agreed. "Make sure you rest. We have a baby to deliver," he teased as he got to his feet. Leaning over, he kissed her forehead, secretly checking for fever before moving to her lips. Lingering there, he nuzzled her nose to nose. "God how I love you, Candice Parker Ford."

Her heart fluttered at the confession, drawing tears to her eyes. "You should go, before I change my mind," she whispered.

"Ok." He straightened himself, smoothing his hair

with his palm. "I'll be home Christmas morning and we'll ring the holiday bells."

"Yes, we will," she agreed, blinking the tears he had induced. "I love you too, Gary."

"I know." He grinned down at her, ready to tear up himself. Touching her raised knee with the tips of his fingers, he turned and marched into the kitchen.

Watching him go, Candy's belly grew tight, and she closed her eyes against the pain. Breathing in deeply, she pushed the breath out through pursed lips, thinking about her last visit with Dr. Castleberry. The contractions were real enough, they just weren't going anywhere, and she hoped that they would stay that way at least until her husband returned.

"Candy, would you like some breakfast?" Carol offered as Holly helped Lanelle into her spot at the table.

"Yeah, I'll come and sit with everyone," Candy agreed, as sulking wouldn't help her mood. "I need to focus on those bells Gary was talking about."

Upstairs, giggles rang out. Now that the two siblings shared a bathroom, they had been rising earlier than they had before. "I'll go," Carol offered.

"I'll serve the plates," Holly added.

Taking a seat next to her mother, Candy leaned over and gave her a half hug. "How do you like the chair?"

"I love it!" Lanelle sang. Accepting her plate, she used her fork to stir her scrambled eggs. "It's a wonderful gift."

"It is," Candy agreed. "For both of us, I think."

Turning to Holly, she changed the subject. "Everyone is coming over to eat all this breakfast, right?"

"Yes. Ben, Eve, and Roger should be here shortly. They spent the evening wrapping presents and they want to arrange them under the tree today."

"That's nice." Candy rubbed her belly. "This Christmas may be all about the family and keeping it safe, but the kids still need a dash of normal."

"Indeed," Lanelle seconded. Crunching a bite of bacon, she looked thoughtful. "Although, my gifts won't be as good. Your in-laws have extravagant tastes."

"Your gifts will be every bit as good," Candy countered, hearing footfalls on the back step. "They're here. Please don't worry, mom."

The rear entrance opened, and the trio clomped inside, Eve and Roger each carrying a large bag of packages.

"Merry Christmas!" Roger bellowed as he closed the portal.

"Grampa," Daks called from upstairs. Rushing to get down, the pair met at the base of the steps, Dakota grabbing his tall legs for a hug.

"Hello, hello." Roger massaged his back until he had had enough and pulled away.

Moving past them, Eve produced brightly wrapped boxes from her sack and arranged them under the tree.

"Do that later, love," Roger commanded. "Breakfast is served. We can eat while it's hot and then place the gifts."

"Hmmph," she grunted, leaving the bag to take her place at the table. "Did all of your packages arrive?"

"All but one," Candy confessed. "Overall, we are set."

"That's good." Roger accepted his plate and sat next to his wife. "There's been so much disappointment this year, we need some things to go right."

Taking the empty chair next to Candy, Ben grinned at Holly as she brought a bright eyed Joylana down. "When do you work again? At the vaccination thing."

"We start back hard the week after Christmas, but I'm planning on being home most of the time after the baby comes." She glanced at Candy, then said more gently, "Are you still having the Braxton-Hicks contractions?"

Her jaw dropping, Candy stared at her. Clamping it shut, she stammered, "I've had a few."

"Yes, I've noticed," Holly informed her with knowing grin.

"What's a Braxton-Hicks?" Ben asked innocently.

"It means she will go into labor soon," Eve interrupted between bites. Folding her hands before her, she glared at her daughter-in-law. "Did you tell Gary before he left?"

"No," Candy replied curtly. "He has enough to worry about. Besides, Melody said they could happen for weeks before the baby comes."

"Exactly," Holly seconded. "We just want to be ready when they become real."

"And how do we know when they're real?" Ben pushed. The whole pregnancy thing lay outside his comfort zone, even if he had taken Candy to her last two appointments with Melody Castleberry. He got a warm and fuzzy feeling in his gut when he thought about the doctor with bright red hair, but so far, she hadn't made use of the number he had bestowed upon her, unfortunately for him.

"They will become regular," Holly explained. "They get stronger as well. She'll know when the time comes," she reassured, giving Candy a nod.

"I hope so," Candy whispered, uncomfortable with the whole conversation.

Luckily, the speculation lulled as everyone enjoyed the hearty breakfast. Once they had finished, they moved to the living area, where Eve returned to the placement of the gifts beneath the tree, which they had decorated the week before. Watching as she worked, Candy could see the perfection Eve seemed to strive for in all things.

While their grandmother worked, Joy and Daks brought out toys, encouraging their grandfather to join them on the floor.

"Woowoos, Grampa," Dakota informed him, assigning him the role of fireman in their game.

Happy to play along, Candy and Ben each accepted a vehicle and soon their path had been laid out from the front room, down the hall, and into the den on the other end of the house. Unable to crawl such a long distance, Candice quickly established herself as the used car lot. Grabbing a good-sized bucket of hot wheels, she lined the edge of the sofa with her selection and declared that she had opened for business.

Giggles filled the air as they played, the game taking them all the way to lunch, which was followed by nap time in their happy home.

"I think I'll go home for a nap myself," Roger announced as the children were taken upstairs.

"I'll go as well," Eve agreed. "I've planned a Zoom meeting with a few of the office staff this afternoon."

"We'll have dinner around six," Carol reminded them.

"Sounds good." Roger pulled on his coat and led his wife out the back door, closing it gently behind them.

"Mind if I camp in the den and watch a bit of television?" Ben asked, knowing that they wouldn't. He had done so several times in the weeks and months since he had joined their bubble, but it never hurt to ask.

"Of course not," Candy teased, ready to join him. Her favorite chair, an old recliner, had also been relegated to the den, and was a good place to nap. The noise of a random movie in the background wouldn't disturb her a bit.

"Oh my God," Candy gasped, clutching the arm of her chair firmly enough to turn her knuckles white.

Observing her in the flickering light of his movie, Ben swallowed. "Are you ok, Candy?" When she didn't respond, he scooted to the chair next to hers. "Hey. Is this one of those fake pains?"

"It's not fake," she grunted, her teeth clenched. "I think my water just broke."

White as a sheet, Benjamin leapt to his feet. "I'll get Holly."

"Call Gary!" Candy practically screamed.

"Yeah, I'm getting Holly," he repeated, darting from the room. Returning with the nurse in tow a moment later, he could see she looked better. "Is it over?"

Candy glared at him. "Did you call Gary?"

"Carol's doing that now," Holly soothed, removing Candy's blanket to examine her clothing. "I'm afraid you're right, your water definitely broke from the look of things."

"Maybe she just wet herself," Ben offered, trying to be helpful.

"We'll know when we get her up," Holly explained. "Help me push the footrest in." Righting the recliner, she offered her hand and Candy used her leverage to get to her feet. As soon as she stood, a gush of water ran down her leg. "That confirms it," Holly deduced. "We need to pull your car around. CAROL!"

"What, love," the housekeeper replied, bouncing into the room.

"We need towels and Candy's hospital bag

ASAP," she commanded. "Ben, go pull your car around back, please."

"My car?" Ben gasped, visualizing his leather seats.

"Yes, we need to go now, unless you want to deliver this baby here."

"I'll get the car," he agreed, dashing from the room.

"I need dry clothes," Candy suggested.

"It wouldn't help," Holly soothed. "Each time you have a contraction, it will just push out more fluid." Glancing at her watch, she marked the time.

"I've got the bag." Caroline rejoined them, her features pensive. "Gary's house is out on a call. Dispatch is going to try and reach them."

Tears filled her eyes as Candy allowed them to guide her down the hall. Accepting her jacket, she hadn't made it to the back door when the next contraction hit. Cursing under her breath, she doubled over, and everyone halted, waiting for it to pass.

When she was free to move again, they got her outside and down the steps where Ben sat in his BMW. In the passenger seat, a nest of fresh towels greeted her. "I'm sorry about your seat," she offered as she climbed in.

"It's ok," he replied anxiously, currently more concerned about making it to the hospital. "You'll ride with us in case we need you, right?" He stared at Holly across Candy's swollen belly, hoping she would agree.

"You have time," Holly replied with a small

giggle. "Go straight to the hospital and drive safely. They are only going to let one person in when you get there," she explained.

"All right." He straightened in his seat, waiting for the door to close and the real journey to begin.

TWELVE

New Arrival

KEEPING THE SPEED DOWN, Benjamin Monroe weaved his way through icy, snow sprinkled streets. Midafternoon, the traffic was light in the midst of the stay-at-home orders. In the seat next to him, Candy groaned, which only made him all the more anxious. "How far apart?"

"I don't know," she grunted.

"I'll time it," he offered, noting the numbers on the digital dash clock. It would give him something to do, at the very least it might prove helpful. His mouth dry, he uttered a muted whistle. "You know, I don't know anything about delivering babies."

"It doesn't matter," Candy spat, the contraction still gripping her. A moment later, it began to ease, and she could breathe easily. "Gary is going to meet us."

"Yeah, Gary will be there," he seconded. Pulling up at a stop light, he stole a sideways glance at his passenger. "Anything I can do?"

"Just drive, Ben," she replied, laughing lightly. "This isn't at all how I picture this going down."

"Pfft, you and me both." The light changed and he applied the gas. Two blocks later, she tensed. "Four minutes," he informed her gently.

"Augh," she replied, struggling to breathe over the top. "Must relax," she panted.

"Should I distract you?"

"Unlikely."

Ben wished he knew more about the process. "We're almost there," he soothed.

The contraction ending, Candy released a long slow exhale. "Thank you for being here."

"Of course." He grinned to himself. "Funny how things turned out. A year ago, we hardly knew each other." The hospital looming ahead, he concentrated on the road, making the final turn, and pulling right up to the doors.

"You can't park here," a security officer shouted.

"Can I make a drop off here?" Ben called back, stepping out of the BMW.

Looking in through the front window, the rent-a-cop grimaced. "Covid?"

"Baby."

"Nu-uh, you need the other campus. Go around the corner and follow the signs. There's a dedicated parking lot. I'll radio over and have a chair brought out for her."

"Thanks." Ben slipped behind the wheel. "We have to go around and park, but he is going to let them know we're coming."

"That's nice of him."

"Yeah. Probably a rough job, especially now." Making the turn, he could see an orderly at the entrance with the chair, and just beyond the parking lot. Pulling into a space, her ride arrived next to them.

"Need a lift?" The young man joked, bringing a brief smile to Candy's lips.

Helping her out of the car, Ben was less amused. "Her water broke. Do you need the towels?"

"Naw, man, just put her in the chair."

Pivoting, Candy transferred to the wheelchair. "Grab my bag, please."

"Yes, ma'am." Ben threw the strap over his shoulder and followed the orderly.

Inside, Candy presented her pre-registration card at the admitting station. Finding it harder to focus on her breathing through her covering, she moaned, "I should have practiced while wearing this mask."

"Maybe they will let you take it off once you get to the room," he offered, adjusting his own.

"Ford!" A nurse called from swinging doors across the room.

Wheeling her up, an upturned hand signaled for them to stop. A pain overtaking her, Candy braced for it, doing her best to breathe through it.

"Will you be accompanying the patient in her delivery?" The nurse addressed her question to Ben.

"No, her husband should be here shortly," Ben stammered. "I'm just a friend."

"You can't go back," she informed him tartly, ready to take the chair.

"Ben!" Candy grunted, terrified at the moment. "Get Dr. Castleberry."

Rolling her eyes, the nursed tossed back, "Wait here."

The contraction had passed by the time Melody came through the swinging doors. "Ben! What are you doing here?" Looking down at her patient, a bewildered expression crinkled her eyes. "Where's Gary?"

"His house was out on a call. They are going to get him here as soon as they can," Candy informed her, feeling another pain coming on. "Crap."

"The rules are explicit. If you want someone with you, they need to be here now," her doctor explained. "Ben can come back with us, or you can go alone, but if Gary isn't here, he is going to miss it."

"You can't make an exception?" Ben demanded, ready to fight for Gary's rights. "He'll be here as quick as he can."

"Unfortunately, no," Melody explained. "Once we go back, the group is set. If you leave, you can't come back, and no one else will be permitted in."

"Please don't leave me!" Candy begged, panting heavily.

"We need to go," Melody announced, indicating for the nurse to take the chair. Glancing at Ben, she hesitated, her lips pursed behind her bright pink mask. "You coming?"

"It doesn't look like I have a choice," he observed. Her bag still over his shoulder, he pushed past her to follow his charge down the hall.

"Thank you for staying," Candy huffed, resting back against her pillow.

"What are friends for?" Ben countered, giving her hand a squeeze. He had quickly gotten over his qualms about the process. Candy needed him, and he intended to be there.

"We're ready to push." Melody informed them, shoving the sheet that covered Candy's lower half back a bit.

"This was fast," Ben observed, noting they had only been at the hospital an hour or so.

"She was almost fully dilated when you arrived," she explained. "If you had waited, you might not have made it."

"Where's Gary?" Candy panted.

"We'll locate him after the baby's delivered. Right now, we have work to do. Now, when the next pain comes, you bear down and push," her doctor firmly instructed.

Doing as she was told, Candy held herself up on shaky arms, curling into her belly and giving it all she had as the next pain clamped down on her. "Augh," she squealed, feeling a gush of water and an odd sensation as her son's tiny body slipped into Dr. Castleberry's practiced hands.

Falling back against the bed, she managed, "I don't feel so good."

"It's ok, Candy. You did it!" Ben massaged her shoulder, congratulating her fondly.

"Ben," she slurred, then she slumped in the sheets as she lost consciousness.

THIRTEEN

What Friends Are For

CANDY SAT in her hospital bed, her son suckling at her breast. The room little more than a cubical, Benjamin Monroe lay sprawled across the only chair in the most uncomfortable position she had ever seen. Hearing a light knock on the door, she flung the sheet up to cover her breast and babe with the thin material.

A privacy curtain hanging between her and the portal, she couldn't see who had entered at such a late hour. Her breath catching when he came into view, she gasped, "Gary!"

"Shh," he hushed her, pulling down his mask to cover her mouth with his. Pressing their foreheads together, he panted, "I'm sorry. They tried to keep me out, but I had to see you."

"It's ok," she whispered back. "It all went fine."

"I know. I did get to talk to Dr. Castleberry," he grunted. "She wouldn't let me come up."

"Yeah, it's against the rules." Candy blinked at

him, noticing he wore plain white scrubs. "You look like an orderly."

"It's my disguise." He winked at her. "I have a few friends here, one of whom helped me in, and hopefully out."

"What's up, buddy?" Ben asked quietly, moaning loudly as he stretched.

"I'm here for a quick check-in," Gary explained, glancing anxiously at the door. "I'm sure I'll end up buying this place a new wing to make amends if I get caught."

Candy snickered. "We're fine, Baby. Don't get in trouble."

"I'll see you tomorrow, I'm sure," he agreed, getting to his feet, he lifted the sheet at the same time so his wife's breast and nursing offspring were exposed. "Looks painful."

"It's going," Candy disagreed. "I'll get used to it. Are you sure I'm getting out tomorrow?"

"Yes. I already took care of the bill and all the paperwork. Melody should make rounds early and release you. Ben, you'll have to bring them home, if that's all right with you."

"What are friends for?" Ben gave his client turned bubble mate a crooked grin before it faded. "We don't have a car seat."

"I left it at the admission desk." Replacing his mask, Gary swished a small wave at his bride. "Sleep well, Kitten."

Candy stared at the swaying curtain, tears filling her eyes. Turning her attention back to her suckling infant, she blinked rapidly, hoping Ben hadn't noticed.

"You need anything?" he asked across the cramped space.

"Nothing you can give me." She sighed, happy he had made it to see them, but terribly sad to see him go. "This damn virus is ruining everything."

"It's not what we wanted, but it isn't ruined," Ben cautioned. "Your son is here and you are both healthy. You can't really ask for more than that."

Candy sniffed, considering the advice. "That's true." Little Gary had dropped the nipple and she moved to hide it as she lifted him to her shoulder. "Yeah, I guess it could be worse," she agreed as she bounced him gently in her practiced arms.

Pulling around to the back of the house, Ben wedged the car as close to the steps as he could, noting Gary had bounded out as soon as they rounded the corner. "You got this?" He called as he climbed from behind the wheel.

"Oh yeah, Daddy's got this," Gary hollered back with a goofy grin. "Go on in and wait with everyone else. Candy and I will bring the baby in shortly. Give me the keys."

Handing over the fob on the way by, Ben did not hesitate, getting out of the cold as quickly as he could.

Candy noted that Ben left them, but to her surprise, her husband climbed into the vacated seat rather than help her out. "Did we need another trip around the block?"

Hearing the fatigue in her voice, Gary started the car. "No, I just want to keep you warm for a sec. We need to talk, Kitten."

A pain jabbing her chest, Candy whispered, "Is it Mom?"

"Oh God, no," Gary spat, laughing anxiously. "Nothing's wrong like that. It's just that I've done something," he confessed. Forcing himself to look at her, his voice deepened. "I wanted you to know before I tell the others."

Her mind racing, Candice Ford could only guess what her husband had done now. "Well, spit it out then," she stated a little more curtly than she had intended. "You know I hate surprises."

"I know, Kitten," he soothed, taking her hand. "But I really didn't think you would mind this one. I know how much you have dreaded the way Mother has pushed to give our son my name." He paused, glancing at her again. "I didn't."

"You didn't," she replied more gently. "You didn't name him Gerald?"

"No. I chose a different name. A person I think we both admire." He inhaled deeply, then gushed, "I named him after your mother, Kitten."

"You named our son Lanelle?" she shrieked.

Bursting into a short laugh, he clarified, "No. I named him Lane. Short from Lanelle."

"Oh my," she breathed, the magnitude of the choice heavy in the air.

"Of course, I also named him Benjamin, because Ben is also someone I think we both look up to, but I figure we will call him Lane." He glanced over his shoulder at the tiny sleeping face. "You make beautiful babies, Candy."

"Let's go in," she suggested, not sure what to say to his impromptu decision and certain their Christmas was about to be anything but merry.

FOURTEEN

What's in a Name

SHUTTING OFF THE ENGINE, Gary helped Candy out of the car, then retrieved their son, taking care to wrap him well before pulling him out into the frosty air. Following her into the house, he held his bundle firmly, relieved he finally held his son in his arms. He had worried so many hours between the news Candy had conceived to that very moment. "Hello, my angel," he breathed once he had Lane inside and could have a better look.

"When do we get to see him?" Roger called from the living room, where the group impatiently waited as Gary dawdled at the kitchen table.

"I'm looking. I haven't gotten to see him yet, either," Gary teased, grinning ear to ear as he inspected the tiny hands. "He's perfect."

Leaving him to his prodding, Candy made her way in, where her favorite spot on the couch had been reserved for her. "You look tired, Mom," she observed as she snuggled into her seat.

"We've been anxious," Lanelle replied briskly.

Candy winced, hating that the others might have worried. "Everything went fine. I know not getting to be there sucks, but we are both healthy and that's what matters." Candy grinned at Ben as she paraphrased his advice to her.

Entering with his newborn, Gary held him up for all to see. "Before we start passing him around, I'd like to introduce our son." His eyes darted around the group and landed on his mother, all listening for what came next. "Benjamin Lane Ford."

"What?" Eve squealed as an audible gasp filled the room.

"You didn't give him your name?" Roger added, taking his wife's shoulders with a firm arm at the same time.

Around them, chaos erupted as the others took up the discussion.

"You named your son after me?" Ben couldn't believe his ears.

"How sweet! No junior for you!" Caroline sang, sidling up to have a better look at the newcomer.

"No, Dad. I didn't think that would suit him or us very well," Gary explained, side stepping those who had gathered around him. Taking a seat on the ottoman, across from his parents, he offered the babe like a sacrifice. "Please try to understand, Mother. I have another son, and I just couldn't bear to do that to him."

"Dakota would never know the difference," Eveline argued.

"No, but I would," Gary stated flatly. An odd silence fell over the group as they considered that sentiment.

Glancing around her, Eve could see how unpopular her side was. Before her, Gary held up her new grandson.

"Grandmother, this is Lane." He offered to let her hold the baby first.

Her cheeks growing brighter, the gesture was not lost on her. "He's a sweet little thing," she murmured, folding her arm with this tiny head in the crook.

"You're calling him Lane?" Lanelle asked, her tone on the meek side. "I'm so honored." Blinking rapidly, a single tear escaped to stain her cheek.

"You'll get to hold him next," Gary promised, giving her an affectionate hug.

"What's in a name, anyway?" Roger snorted, using a finger to tease baby lips.

"You're going to wake him," Eve scolded.

"Yes, I want to see his eyes," her husband explained.

"I'm sure you will get to see them at some point." Candy cackled. They acted as if they had never seen a baby before, but recalling how they had behaved when they brought Joylana home she could see nothing had changed.

Hours later, those from across the street began the trek home. Climbing into her new chair, Lanelle announced she wanted to join them.

"What's going on across the street?" Candy demanded when Holly put Joylana's jacket on her while Caroline buttoned Dakota.

"It's your anniversary, silly girl," Holly hissed.

"Oh my God." She had forgotten. "Things happened so fast with little man, I have no clue what day it is."

"It's Christmas Eve. We are taking the kids for the night, and we'll bring them over early for Santa," Carol suggested.

"Right. That's a brilliant plan," Gary approved. Hoisting the newborn to his shoulder, he mocked, "Too bad this one is still on the tit, or he could go too!"

"Gary, how rude!" Candy chastised, giving his arm a solid punch.

"I'm only teasing," he jeered.

A few minutes later, the couple watched from the front glass as the parade made it down their driveway and crossed the deserted street. Candy laughed when her mother made a few donuts in the road before turning into the drive and taking her new ramp to their sliding glass door.

"I can't believe it has all worked out," she confessed, leaning her head against the arm she had just pretended to injure.

"Of course it worked out," Gary shot back. "Ford Family Christmas is the best time of the year."

"Well, I'm afraid there won't be any lovemaking for this anniversary," she teased.

"Oh, Kitten," he whispered, nuzzling her with his nose. "You and I are always making love. The best kind, in fact."

"What kind is that?" she playfully scoffed.

"The kind that melts my heart, then sets it on fire. The kind that can't be explained and yet doesn't need to be."

"Poetry," she teased, amazed he could make her feel so good with so little effort.

"With you? Always." He kissed her, his warm lips gently searching, then pulling away. "Happy anniversary, Mrs. Ford."

Her lids fluttering, Candy gasped. "I don't see how you do that," she observed, breathless.

"Magic." Stepping back, he indicated the path to the second floor. "Let's go upstairs and get our new arrival settled in."

"You're such a romantic." She giggled, sauntering past. For a year to have been so wrong, everything on this night felt so right.

FIFTEEN

A Toast to 2020

CURLED IN THEIR BED, Candy's head rested in the crook of her husband's arm. Next to them in his bassinet, Lane's breathing carried faintly through the air, bringing a smile to her lips. Hearing him stir, she knew their slumber would be interrupted shortly. Extricating herself as kindly as she could, she made a visit to the bathroom before lifting her son to offer a feeding.

Still wrapped in the sheets, Gary stretched in an exaggerated manner. "What time is it?"

"Early," Candy replied. Catching the sound of the door below them, she corrected, "Scratch that."

"I hear them," Gary agreed. "I'll put on some clothes."

"I'm going to feed this little guy, so take your time."

Throwing off the covers, Gary opted for a quick shower, then donned clean jeans and a festive green and black plaid flannel shirt. Taking the baby, he crossed to the nursery to change him while Candy also dressed.

"I assume this little elf suit is for today?"

"Yes." She had purchased it and a slew of other items in the last few months. "Thank goodness for online shopping and home delivery, or the poor little guy would be stuck in Joy's old clothes." She chuckled, picturing at the amount of pink and lavender clothing her daughter had worn.

"Hey, real men wear pink," Gary informed her, holding him up for inspection. "What do you think?"

"I think it's adorable. Thank you."

"You bet, Kitten. I love being the daddy." He grinned ear to ear as he lay Lane into her arms so she could wrap him in a thin blanket.

Finally, ready to face the day, the pair quietly crept down the stairs, expecting to find a living room filled with chaos.

Instead, Joylana and Dakota where nowhere to be seen. Lanelle and Roger sat at the kitchen table while Carol was busily making breakfast.

"Where is everyone?" Candy gasped.

"Mommy!" Daks answered her question with a shout, Joy close behind as they darted in from the den. "Baby 'ane Christmas," he sang as he clutched at her waist and craned his neck to see.

Behind them followed Eve, who had been entertaining them until the couple joined them. "We waited for you. Daks wanted to be sure Lane got his presents, too."

Nodding her understanding, Candy mumbled her thanks, then turned her attention to the doting big brother. "Let me sit, and you can see him." Taking her favorite seat on the couch, she lay the baby out onto her legs and grinned.

"Baby 'ane, so pretty," Dakota announced. His hand gentle as a feather, he caressed his brother's tiny cheek. "Joy'ana, come see!"

Across the room, the two-year-old had little interest in the new baby. Instead, she had begun inspecting packages, as if she could tell by the wrapping who they belonged to.

"Let me help you, sweetheart," Eve offered. Wearing a simple knit pantsuit, she sat on the floor and crossed her legs in a most undignified manner.

"Are you feeling all right?" Candy asked.

"I'm fine," Eve sniped. She and Joy often played together since her arrival at the house across the street. Choosing to focus on the special morning, she ignored the question her daughter-in-law probably wanted to ask. "Here, Joy, let Grandmother help you."

The toddler had chosen a package and, as if it were a chair, plopped her rear onto Eveline's lap to open it. Picking up her phone from the end table, Candice clicked a few pictures as the gifting commenced.

Seeing that he trailed behind, Dakota abandoned the cooing and went straight for the bigger boxes. The sound of gleeful children drew the others into the room, and Gary presented his bride with a steaming cup of coffee when he joined her.

"This is nice," he observed, settling onto the cushion next to hers.

"Very nice," she agreed, followed by a noisy sip. "Of all the fears Christmas has brought me, the year I thought should be the scariest has turned out to be the best."

"Indeed." Eveline's voice was crisp as she cut her eyes over at her daughter-in-law.

Stroking his chin thoughtfully, Gary pondered his mother along with the others who were part of their bubble. Across the room, Benjamin Monroe leaned against the kitchen doorframe, grinning like a fool at the mess before him. On the ottoman sat his father. Each new unwrapped toy had to be shared with him, as Dakota obviously adored his Grampa.

"What's this?" Caroline asked, lifting one of Joy's presents for all to see. "Did Joylana get big girl panties for Christmas?"

"Oh, no," Candy groaned. "Who did that?"

"What?" Gary defended with a shrug. "It's time for her to start, don't you think?"

"I suppose." His wife sighed. "I mean if she's ready. That's not something you can force. Or rush."

"You just want to keep her a baby," Holly teased, peeking over at the sleeping infant on her employer's lap. "Mind if I hold him?"

"Not at all." Lifting him, Candy passed him over to eager hands. Resting back into the plush seat, she sighed. "She will always be my baby. I know they have to grow up, though." Glancing at Gary, she grinned. "And we have a new baby to dote on…for a little while."

Clasping her fingers between his, Gary kissed the back of her hand. Releasing his grip, he stood and offered the seat to Holly. "You can sit with him. I need to stand for a bit."

Taking him up on his generosity, their nurse sat between Candy and Lanelle. "Did you see Joy's new baby dolls?"

"I did. Did you pick those out for her?" Candy replied.

Sitting up straight, Eve pursed her lips. "I did. I thought it was time she had a few girl toys."

"Girl toys?" Ben asked innocently.

"Yes. Dolls and houses, things like that," Eve defended evenly.

"And if Daks wants to play with them?" Gary asked with a shrug. "You know he will want to share."

"Then he can play, too." Eve's features softened. "I did not mean to imply there was anything wrong with her playing trucks and cars, or Daks having a few dolls, but I for one might like to play dress up once in a while."

A short silence followed before loud boisterous laughter filled the small space. "So, what you are saying, Mother…is that *you* want to play dolls."

Sniffing loudly, Eve tightened her jaw. "With my granddaughter, yes." Eyeing a large box in the back, she cringed, knowing they would soon unwrap the tea set and tiny table, and the ribbing would start again.

Shaking her head, Candy grinned. "Thank you, Eve. I'm sure she —and you—will enjoy them very much."

Glancing around at the others, Eve sighed. She never had been good at making friends, and even her family held her at arm's length most of the time. It didn't mean she didn't love them, she just needed figure out how to say so. Stroking Joylana's back, she leaned in and whispered, "Let's open the big box. Grandmother has a special surprise for you!"

Continuing with the unwrapping, the group worked their way through the remainder of the gifts, discovering all sorts of new treasures. When they were done, the children played with their new toys, mingling and showing them off to their elders until lunch was served.

"An excellent meal, Caroline," Eveline praised. Seated around the dining room table, the Ford family bubble lingered over dessert, wine, and good conversation.

Glancing around at the group from the head of the table, Gary exhaled loudly. Pushing back his chair, he stood and raised his glass. "Ladies and gentlemen, I know that bellies are full, and napping stations are calling. But before we go our separate ways for an afternoon of rest and digestion, I hope that I might make a toast."

Smiling up at her husband, Candy shook her head. "You Fords and your ceremonies." Glancing at Eve, she noted how calm the older woman appeared. She had half expected a tantrum over Lane's name that morning, but the older woman seemed rather sedate. Dressed almost casually, she had played on the floor, no less. Perhaps living with them in the bubble had finally softened a few of Eveline Ford's rough edges.

"No ceremony." Gary laughed, "only a heartfelt desire to convey my feelings for this wonderful group of people gathered here today. You see, 2020 began like any other year. We were busy. Each of us going and blowing in umpteen different directions. But then something unimaginable happened."

"The quarantine," Lanelle muttered.

"Yes. Covid came and changed all our lives forever. We've been fortunate, though. None of us have become ill. We all have friends outside, and some of them were not so lucky." He paused, and the air grew heavy. "But that's not really what I wanted to share."

Continuing, he gently shook his glass his glass. "I want to make a toast. To Benjamin Monroe. I'm not even sure how you ended up here, but I'm glad you're here. You went from practicing family law, to live-in gardener, electrician, and chauffer. From being some guy I knew, to part of our family. I never had a brother, but if I did, I think he would be something like you. Here's to Ben." He raised his glass, then took a long sip.

"Is that why you named your son after me?" Ben laughed at the thought of it, shaking his head before accepting the toast, taking a sip of his own.

"He named him after me," Lanelle pointed out. "They are calling him Lane."

"He is named for both of you," Gary countered. "To the mother and brother who were not born to me, but both of whom I love very much."

"Hear hear," Roger boomed, raising his glass high. Getting to his feet, he bowed slightly in Gary's direction. "May I?"

Hesitant, not intending to make too much of the occasion, Gary forced a smile. "Sure, Dad. What's your toast?"

"I'm going to toast 2020. Perfect vision they call it, and I dare say this year has given us that. What was once held in great importance now has taken a back seat. To each and every one of you and the time we have shared that never would have been."

"How thoughtful," Eve grunted. Standing, she didn't wait for permission. "To my grandchildren, whom I have played harder with and enjoyed more in the last two months than I did in the last two years." Lowering her glass, she toyed with the bottom, as if searching for the words. "This group never ceases to amaze me. I may have been hard to get here, but it has been a genuine pleasure to live among you."

"Hear hear," Candy toasted, expecting the end, but Roger seemed to only be warming up, reclaiming his turn.

"To my lovely wife, for agreeing to come here,

and for the graceful way she has learned to accept the things she cannot change."

Holly and Caroline snickered, and Candy caught Gary's eye, who waved her off with a slight flick of his wrist. The couple were amusing after all, so why stop them so soon?

Eve's turn, she dove in, "To my beautiful daughter-in-law, who makes my son very happy. And to Ben, Caroline, and Holly. You each are wonderful people, and we are grateful you have shared your home with us." She took another long drink, emptying her glass.

Blinking a few times, Lanelle had been enjoying the back-and-forth nature of their toasts, noting that it would be time to hear something about her. Fixing her gaze on their patriarch, she waited with bated breath.

Roger, noting the anticipation in her eyes, slowly nodded. "I haven't forgotten you, Lanelle. For I understand fully why my son has chosen you for his son's name sake. May our new grandchild be as dear, loving, and giving as we have found you to be." He raised his glass and waited for the others to join.

"Well, I believe we have toasted our glasses dry," Gary observed, hoping they had gotten to the bottom of things.

Still standing, Eve picked up the bottle and freshened her glass, then her husband's. "We have more, do we not?"

"I'll get another bottle," Carol replied as she left the room.

Taking his seat, Gary scratched his head, cutting

his eyes over to his wife. Taking that as her cue, Candy raised her glass. "I wouldn't mind a turn. I would like to toast my in-laws, but I'm afraid I haven't rehearsed anything fancy to say. Only that I know that Daks and Joy both love having you here. I'm glad you came." Taking a sip, she smiled at Ben. "I would toast you, as well, but Gary did such a wonderful job I don't think I can top it. Instead, I will thank you. Taking me to my appointments and then being there for my delivery…" her voice cracked, and she swallowed hard. "Thank you, Ben."

"You are more than welcome, Candy," he replied gently.

The new bottle arrived, and glasses were refilled, but the moment seemed broken by the honesty of Candy's words. Sitting in her chair once more, Eve tapped the rim of her glass gently with an extended finger. Finally, she raised it slightly, "To our new baby, Lane." Taking a large swallow, she watched as the others reluctantly followed suit. "This isn't really a toast, either, but I do have something to say on the subject."

"Oh, God. Here it comes," Candy muttered, gripping the arm of her chair.

"I know," Eve spat, glaring at her. "I'm a crotchety old woman." Her voice quavered, and her eyes teared, causing her to dab at them with her napkin. "I made such a fuss about giving him Gary's name that there is no graceful way out for me. Therefore, I will eat a little crow. I think that Benjamin

Lane is a lovely name. Not so lovely as Gerald Ford Junior would have been, but that is your choice to make." A small smile forming on her lips, Eve sighed. "Quite honestly, I appreciate that you stand up to me, Candice. Not many people do."

Candy winced. "The name was really Gary's idea. I had nothing to do with it."

"But you didn't like my choice," Eve insisted. "And that you said so took courage. Someday, we won't be on opposite sides of every issue," she finished firmly, gulping from her glass and ready to go home.

"Yes, not having to disagree about everything would be nice," Candy whispered, sipping from hers.

Taking that as a good ending, Gary stood. "Well, a fine Christmas this has been. I don't think we need to linger any longer."

In the bassinet, Lane stirred, and Candy welcomed the opportunity to leave the group. Lifting her son, she cooed, "Let's go have some dinner for you, little man." Glancing at Eve, she noted the flush on her mother-in-law's cheeks and added, "Thank you, Eveline. I know that was hard for you to say. And for the record, we love you, too." She straightened, bouncing the baby slightly. "I love you, too." Waiting for Eve to meet her gaze, she smiled at her. "Lane and I are going up stairs if you would care to join us."

Surprised at the offer, Eve hesitated, torn by the desire to accept. "I would like that, Candice. But I'm afraid I have a tea date with my granddaughter."

Candy grinned, secretly quite pleased with the woman's choices in gifts this year. "You two have a wonderful time," she commanded, briefly patting the older woman's arm as she passed by on her way out the door.

Epilogue

ARRIVING at her apartment after a long day at the hospital, Dr. Melody Castleberry let herself in and flicked on a light. A comfortable two-bedroom town-house, she had lived alone for near on a decade. Not even an animal stirred in the quiet space, as caring for one with her erratic schedule had never been possible.

The same with relationships. At least that's what Melody told herself every time she got the urge to say yes to a date. So far, it had worked, too. She had kept away even the most dedicated pursuer.

However, Benjamin Monroe had not been dedicated in any sense of the word. He had delivered Candice Ford to her office twice, both times all business. Noting the folded piece of paper on her dresser, she wrapped her favorite robe around her and tied the waist. Picking up the note, she ran her thumb across the dried ink, as if to smudge it. Laying it gently back on the flat surface she studied the curves of his penmanship.

His name and phone number; that's all that he had written. Grinning to herself, she thought about the day they had delivered Candy's baby. It had only taken an hour, but she had gotten to know him. Typically, the men in her birthing chambers were attached, obviously, but under the strange circumstances, this one had been completely single.

Ben had been terrified. But he had shown his true colors, giving it his all when his friend's wife needed him. She could tell herself things were good the way they were, but on nights like this, she wasn't so sure. She had no intention of ever making the call when she had accepted his offering, but she didn't throw it away either, leaving her open to this moment.

Snatching it up, she gripped the slip of paper as if a gust of wind might rip it from her fingers. Dialing her phone, she curled her bare feet beneath her on her sofa as she listened to it ring.

"Hello?" Ben's deep voice greeted.

"Hi, Ben," she breathed into the device. "It's Melody. Dr. Castleberry."

"Why, good evening!" The enthusiasm in his masculine tones pulled at her. "I had decided you had pitched me in the trash."

"No," she replied quickly, liking the way he teased her. She had noticed that he had an easy-going personality the night Lane was born. "I needed to let you simmer," she playfully replied.

"Wow."

He paused, creating an awkward silence. Filling

it, she gushed, "Well, you know these are unusual times."

"Very unusual," he agreed. "I would ask you to dinner, but everything is pretty chaotic these days. We would have to find the right place."

"That would be against the rules, really. Meeting in person would." In her mind's eye, she could see his handsome features, her face growing warm. "We could eat outside somewhere…if you don't mind the cold."

They both laughed, dropping the tension. More relaxed, Melody asked, "Have you returned to your apartment yet?"

"No, actually I have not. I've decided I'm going to clear it out and stay here with the girls until I'm ready to buy a house."

"A house!" She tapped her lips with an extended finger, remembering distant times. "That sounds nice," she added like an afterthought.

"It will be," he observed. "You want to switch to Zoom or Skype?"

"Oh, no!" The mere mention of something more intimate than an ordinary phone call terrified her. "I really can't talk long," she lied flatly.

"All right then," he soothed, as if he could see her petrified expression. "In that case, maybe we can make a date of it and you can pencil me into that busy schedule of yours."

Her hand resting against her chest, Melody felt her heart beating wildly within her chest. Swallowing her fear, she forced her mind to contemplate the occasion. "I'll be free on Saturday. You can call me back at this number and we can arrange a video chat."

"Sounds lovely," he cooed through the speaker.

"Thank you, Ben," she whispered. Pulling the device away from her ear, she ended the call, then squeezed the phone firmly. She had been alone far too long. It wasn't healthy to hide herself away, no matter how badly things had gone in her last relationship.

Thank You

Thank you for reading, and I hope that you have enjoyed the 2020 installment of the Sweet Christmas Series. Look for a new adventure for Gary and Candy at Christmas next yet. ~ Sam

Books in this series include:
Christmas Candy (2015)
Christmas Eve (2016)
Christmas Carol (2017)
Christmas Joy (2018)
Christmas Holly (2019)
Christmas Lane (2020)

About the Author

Anyone who knows me could tell you, I am a friendly kind of person, never met a stranger and take up conversations anywhere at any time. I work hard, and my mind never seems to shut down, as I wake up often in the middle of the night with ideas pouring out and demanding to be dealt with. Of course that means much of my books were written in the middle of the night.

I grew up and still live in the great state of Texas where everything is bigger, where we have warm weather and a central location. I love my state, my town, and my family, which includes my four sons, my significant other, and many friends as well.

I have thoroughly enjoyed writing this story and hope that you will love reading it just as much. And of course, there will be many more adventures to come.

You can follow Samantha Jacobey at:
Facebook: facebook.com/SamJacobey
Twitter: twitter.com/SamJacobey

Also by SAMANTHA JACOBEY

A New Life Series – an epic adventure, TORI FARRELL's life IS one wild story... escaped from a biker gang and running from drug lords... used by the FBI and hoping to protect her present from her past... IT'S DARK - IT'S BRUTAL, and it's WORTH EVERY MINUTE OF IT!! (Mature read, 18+ for graphic sexual content and violence, including rape)

Summer Spirit Novella Series - no one EVER had a summer romance like this… Charlie visits another plane, parallel to our own, where Summer Angels and Dark Angels battle over the fate of man. A unique twist on an old idea that will keep you guessing; will Charlie and Clarisse ever find their HEA? (New adult)

Teach Me to Prey – in this standalone thriller, JASON TRUITT and his friends have gotten their way for years. Deceit, sex, and foul play aren't normally covered in the curriculum, but they're doing whatever it takes to get under BECKY STEWART's skin. When one of the boys turns up dead, it's a race against time to save the others; a STUNNING STORY that will get your heart racing and leave you breathless by the end… (New Adult)

The Binding (Unexpected Magic #1) - One cursed diary will change two strangers forever...Can Meri and Rider use her mother's old book to figure out why someone is after them? Or will the guilty party succeed, ripping the tome away before killing them and then slithering back into the darkness… (New Adult)

The Wicked Awakened (Unexpected Magic #2) – a Halloween novel; a five-hundred-year-old witch wants to turn SARAH MATTHEWS' body into her new home… A twisted tale involving a coven hell bent on seeing that she succeeds. Who will come out on top in this epic battle of wills? (Mature read, 18+ for graphic sexual content and violence)

The Irrevocable Series - From affluent beginnings, BAILEY DEWITT's life has become a broken mess... after her parents died unexpectedly, she didn't think it could get any worse. But when the arrogance of man catches up and puts the entire world into a dooms-day spiral, there will be only ONE PLACE she can run to - the ONE PLACE she wanted desperately to escape. (New Adult)

The Dragon of Eriden Series - Amicia Spicer led a simple life, until she discovered it had all been a lie… On her deathbed, Arely Spicer confessed to her only daughter that she had been found by, not born to her mother and father. Sad news to be certain, the idea of having a family of flesh and blood waiting to be reunited sent the young, independent woman on the adventure of a lifetime. Little did she know, a dragon's heart beat within her chest and her journey would be more perilous than she could have imagined... (New Adult)

Also from the Lavish Family

The City: The Jane Harvest
A. Nicky Hjort
https://www.lavishpublishing.com/authors/
nicky-hjort-1/

A dystopian thriller… welcome to the future, or at least one possible future...

Winning battles means Ink honors, prestige, and life itself. …Yet nobody understands what losing truly means.

On another planet two hundred years in the future, twenty-one-year-old Isla Jane struggles helplessly to figure out who she is and what her world really means. Marked with a forbidden tattoo of the rising sun, she is a natural champion of humanity and a gifted warrior in Heats– lavish battles fought in the conjoined minds of the participants for the morbid amusement of the masses.

Despite Isla's desire to fade into the background, she emerges as an obvious leader of her people when the senseless assassination of a youth forces her to face the truth. Her volatile world, disguised by its elaborate battles and constant mayhem, is a prison without bars and a coffin, the lid already half-closed, that they must escape.

But when she vows to find a way to bring her people back home, Isla will have to deconstruct consciousness and the very nature of the space time continuum to unravel good from evil, truth from lies, and survival from true love.

Welcome to the City—where it takes lives to save lives…

Fairfield Corners Series
L.A. Remenicky
https://books2read.com/FCSet

Small town romance with a paranormal twist! Each in standalone style, read and enjoy any order, any number!

Saving Cassie – Book 1: Some secrets are too dangerous to keep.

After ten years in the big city, Cassie Holt is back in Fairfield Corners. She may look like the same girl who left home a decade before but she's hiding a dark truth from everyone. When her life is threatened by the demons of her past, her best friend—who happens to be the local sheriff—offers his help.

Deputy Logan Miller has been burned by love. He's not looking to get involved but duty calls when the sheriff tasks him with Cassie's protection. Thrown into close quarters with the gorgeous bookseller, sparks fly. Logan is drawn to Cassie, but it's hard to get close to someone who keeps themselves guarded all the time.

To keep Cassie safe, Logan must open his heart but that's something he swore he'd never do.

Ragan's Song – Book 2: One look into his eyes told her she was in trouble – again!

Ragan returned home to celebrate her parent's anniversary hoping they would forgive her the secrets she's kept from them over the last few years. When she discovered that Adam was still living in Fairfield Corners she hoped her secrets were safe, secrets that drove her away three years, secrets that could change both their lives forever.

Adam Bricklin was devastated when Ragan Newlin left town. No note, no email, no text. She was just gone. It has taken three years for Adam to finally move past the heartbreak he suffered when Ragan left town. Now he's moved on and everything was going well until the day Ragan returned to Fairfield Corners. Now the melody that he lost all those years ago is back. It's the same tune he heard that tells him right from wrong—the one that sang Ragan was the one.

Even separation can't silence Adam and Ragan's song, and now that she's back it's time for Adam to decide if he should let the song die or breathe life into it once again.

Where There's Faith – Book 3: A past she can't remember. A love he can't forget.

After losing everything in an accident that he can only blame himself for, Robbie Newlin embraced sobriety and tried to live his life quietly alone at this family's cottage on the lake. Grief being his only ally, Robbie was perfectly content with how he lived until Faith moved into the cottage next door. Now Faith had him questioning whether to keep grieving or to open his broken heart to let love in again.

Faith McMillan had no memory of her life before that day three years ago. The physical scars had faded but the emotional ones were still fresh and raw. Living rent-free seemed like a great way to finish her second book and give her the time to figure out her next move, but then she met the reclusive guy next door and everything changed.

To get past the broken parts, Robbie and Faith must figure out if they want to continue living their lives in solitude or take a chance on finding an ending together.

www.ingramcontent.com/pod-product-compliance
Lightning Source LLC
Chambersburg PA
CBHW051252170626
46809CB00004B/1606